Praise for *Here We Are*

'A magical piece of writing: the work of a
novelist on scintillating form.'
*The Guardian*

'With a wizardry of his own, Swift conjures
up an about-to-disappear world and turns it into
something of wider resonance.'
*Sunday Times*

'There's nothing extravagant or showy about
*Here We Are* . . . The book's power comes precisely from
the fact that it performs its magic in front of your eyes, leaving
nowhere to hide . . . you wonder how he does it.'
*Financial Times*

'As with all his books, it's the moments of quiet,
undramatic poignancy that stay with you.'
*Sunday Express*

'It is perhaps too simple to say that Swift creates a form
of fictional magic, but what he can do with a page is out
of the ordinary, far beyond most mortals' ken.'
*The Herald*

DI040568

# Here We Are

Graham Swift

SCRIBNER
LONDON NEW YORK SYDNEY TORONTO NEW DELHI

First published in Great Britain by Scribner, an imprint of
Simon & Schuster UK Ltd, 2020
This paperback published in Great Britain by Scribner, an imprint of
Simon & Schuster UK Ltd, 2021

1 3 5 7 9 10 8 6 4 2

Simon & Schuster UK Ltd
1st Floor
222 Gray's Inn Road
London WC1X 8HB

www.simonandschuster.co.uk
www.simonandschuster.com.au
www.simonandschuster.co.in

Simon & Schuster Australia, Sydney
Simon & Schuster India, New Delhi

A CIP catalogue record for this book
is available from the British Library

Paperback ISBN: 978-1-4711-8896-1
eBook ISBN: 978-1-4711-8895-4

Typeset by M Rules
Printed and bound by CPI Group (UK) Ltd, Croydon, CR0 4YY

*For Candice*

It's life's illusions I recall

*Joni Mitchell*

Jack paused in the wings. He knew how to delay his entrance by just the critical number of seconds. He was calm. He was twenty-eight, but he was already a veteran, twelve years on stage, not counting a year and a half in the army. Timing was in the blood, think about it and you were lost.

He patted his bow tie, raised a hand to his mouth and politely cleared his throat, as if about to do no more than enter a room. He smoothed back his hair. Now that the house lights were down he could hear the gradually thickening murmur, like something coming to a boil.

It did not happen very often, but now it happened. The sudden giving way of his stomach, the panic, vertigo, revulsion. He did not have to do this thing: turn into someone else. It posed the paralysing question of who he was in the first place, and the answer was simple. He was nobody. Nobody.

And where was he? He was nowhere. He was on a flimsy structure built over swirling water. Normally he didn't think about it. Now his own legs might have turned to useless struts of rusting iron, clamped in sand. Above all there was the concern that no one should see this, know that he suffered in this way.

No one ever would. In fifty years no one ever would.

He checked his flies for the fourth or fifth time, so that now it was a mere fingering of the air.

He needed someone to push him, to give the brutal shove in his back. Only one person could ever do it: his mother. No one would ever know this either. Every night, every time, still her unseen shove. He barely noticed it and barely thought to thank her.

Where was she tonight? As far as he knew, she was with a man called Carter, her second husband she called him, a garage owner in Croydon. And good luck to her. But it hadn't stopped her giving him, all these years, her invisible push in the back. Sometimes even, he imagined, invisible again among the seats in the dark, her watching, approving eye.

That's my Jack, that's my brilliant boy.

A garage owner—called Carter. I ask you, folks, I ask you. There was a theatre in Croydon called The Grand. He had played there, pantomime. Buttons. Had she come, secretly, with Mr Carter—smelling of car engines and thinking: Bloody Cinderella? That's my boy Jack.

Now he was a boy of twenty-eight and already an old stager, wearing like a second skin this black-and-white get-up that was the outdated rig of showmen, conmen, masqueraders everywhere. These days they were wearing jeans and leather jackets, and twanging guitars. Well, that had come too late for him. For him it was the cane and the boater and the tap shoes. 'And now, folks—don't scream too loudly, girls—it's the sensational Rockabye Boys!' As if he were their fucking uncle. But he had the looks (he knew it), the grin and the lock of hair—he swept it back again—that could flop forward and knock 'em dead (on and off stage, incidentally).

If he could just get on stage in the first place.

As for her 'first husband', there was a man who was truly nobody, truly nowhere: his father. But in between—and it had been a long in-between—she had gone on stage herself, what a cruel bastard business. Think about it and you were lost. And who did she have to push her?

No one must see this, no one must know. He could

3

hear the rising murmur waiting to engulf him. He must breathe, breathe. 'Don't cry, Cinders.' Now he had only himself to push himself, but how was he to do it? Cross the line, step over the edge.

Jack was compere that season (his second) and Ronnie and Evie had the first spot after the interval. It was thanks to Jack that they were in the show at all, and the first spot after the interval was a good one to have. When everything changed, fell apart that August they moved up to last spot of all, not counting Jack's own end-of-show routine.

They'd moved by then up the billing too. People were coming specially to see them. The billboards even started to carry pasted-on fliers with such stuff as 'Come and See with Your Own Eyes!' Jack had said, 'Who else's eyes would it be then?' But his quips weren't so many by those days. His public quips continued. Have you heard the one about the garage owner's wife? The show must go on.

'You're in Brighton, folks, so bloody well brighten up!'

It went on through to early September, and the public only saw the marvel of the thing, the talked-about thing. Then the show was over and the talked-about thing was no more than that, it could only ever exist in the memories of those who'd seen it, with their own eyes, in those few summer weeks. Then those memories would themselves fade. They might wonder anyway if they really had seen it.

Other things were over too. Ronnie and Evie, having had a remarkable debut, coming from nowhere to achieve summer fame and having secured for themselves, it would seem, future bookings, even a whole career, never appeared on stage again. Ronnie never appeared again at all.

According to Eddie Costello, one of the local 'Arts and Entertainments' hacks, writing only a month or so before, the couple—and they were a real couple—had 'taken Brighton by storm'. Possibly overstated at the time, it was now only half the story and no longer a mere Arts and Entertainments one.

Evie finally took off her engagement ring. It had been another case of the show must go on. In the days when his quips were free in coming Jack had cracked that they were engaged to do the summer season, they didn't have to get engaged to each other too. Though clearly they had. The engagement ring, with its single sparkling gem, was even a visible complement—tiny but visible—to her silvery costume. How would it have looked if she'd taken it off before the show came to an end? And it was, like any such ring, a guarantee. If it all worked out, and surely it would, they would get married that September when the show closed and take a honeymoon—preferably not in Brighton.

Or perhaps Evie had hoped that by carrying on wearing the ring the whole thing might revert to what it had been. Everything might be redeemed. She hadn't given it back to Ronnie. Ronnie hadn't asked for it back. He hadn't said anything. Let the ring itself decide.

One day that September, after the show had finished and after the police had said she was free to leave Brighton, she did the obvious thing. She went to the end of the pier, took off the ring and threw it in the sea. She never told Jack. Even then she'd thought, without knowing how her life would turn out, that doing this with the ring might somehow have brought everything back. Might even have brought Ronnie back.

It was a regular seaside holiday show. Variety. Anything from acrobats to the up-and-coming Rockabye Boys to the no longer up-and-coming yet ample Doris Lane, sometimes known as the 'Mistress of Melody', sometimes (in cheeky reference to one of her rivals) as the 'Forces Fiancée'. Anything from jugglers and plate-spinners to 'Lord Archibald', who came on holding a large teddy bear—'hand up its arse' as Jack put it—which he would talk to, and the teddy bear would talk back with a considerable gift for repartee. Throughout that season they would hold conversations on the unfolding state of the world—what Macmillan should have said to Eisenhower and so on. On occasion they might even 'become' Macmillan and Eisenhower, or Khrushchev and de Gaulle. It was the funniest thing, a teddy bear talking like General de Gaulle.

But it was all held together by Jack as compere. The impression was that it was his show. They came to be taken under his wing and it wouldn't have been the same without him. Your pal for the night, your host with the most. Off stage he'd say he was just the oil in the wheels—the oilier the better. But it was no small task.

He was Jack Robinson in those days, as in 'before you can say'. Some patter, some gags, some of them smutty, a bit of singing, some dancing, some tapping of his heels. He did the introductions and links, but also a few numbers of his own and always appeared at the end to wind up the show and do his farewell routine.

The important thing was to send them all out with their

holiday mood endorsed, feeling they'd had their money's worth, they'd had a good time, making them even feel they might sing and dance a bit themselves. For many of them, an evening at the pier show was the highlight.

'And so, folks, this is your old mate Jack Robinson saying goodnight and sweet dreams, whoever she is. And here's a little song to see you on your way. I think you know which one it is. Maestro—if you please!

*When the red, red robin . . .'*

If the audience felt so moved, they might sing along. Or when they went out, to the lights and the sound and smell of the sea again, they might indeed find themselves, as they strolled with happy feet along the boards, singing in their heads, or even out loud, snatches of that song.

*I'm just a kid again doing what I did again!*

It was August 1959.

When Ronnie and Evie moved to final spot, pipping even the Rockabye Boys, Jack's goodnight routine became, in more ways than one, a little trickier. Why had Ronnie and Evie moved to final spot? Because, while the show must go on, there was another theatrical law that said: save till last anything that might be hard to follow. But not to have had Jack's closing number would have been unthinkable, even changed the nature of the show. So on he would come, after all the applause for Ronnie and Evie had died away, having to adapt his farewell patter. He would have his hands raised and pressed together, as if having shared the applause, or in prayerful salute. He would get out his white handkerchief to mop his brow. He would put a sly twist on his having been upstaged.

'Well didn't I tell you, boys and girls, didn't I say? Now all you've got is me. Back down to earth, eh?'

He would drape the handkerchief over his hand and shake it, as if giving it commands. He would turn to the audience and shrug.

The note of clownish companionship was struck. They were in his palm again. It was a skill. Even in those days you could see the man was not just good looks and greasepaint.

Eddie Costello, who was to go on to write for the *News of the World*, would always claim he'd seen it, even if at the time it was Ronnie and Evie he'd picked out.

In the dressing room Ronnie and Evie, turning back into their normal selves, might hear the band striking up and the audience singing along with Jack. They would not sing along themselves. They might not even speak to each other. Or they might try to. The audience who had seen them, only moments ago, bringing about a wonder, would not guess at this off-stage inadequacy.

Years, even decades later, when Jack had long since ceased to be Jack Robinson—who could even remember that fleeting figure?—when he was just Jack Robbins again, though some spoke of his one day being *Sir* Jack Robbins, he was apt to say in interviews, with lordly modesty, 'Actor? Oh, just an old song-and-dance man me.' And he could still sing to himself, playing the part, his one-time song. *Wake up, wake up, you sleepy head!* And he could still give, if he wished, his end-of-the-pier wink and flashing grin, both fully visible and almost catchable from the back row.

Jack, Ronnie and Evie could often have been seen that summer in the Walpole Arms. They would form a lopsided trio, Jack and the couple, or, more often, a lopsided group of four—Ronnie and Evie, the engaged couple, and Jack with whatever compliant but temporary girl, name soon to be forgotten, might happen at that point to be hanging on his arm.

Now, as August moved towards September, neither the threesome nor foursome was in evidence. If Ronnie and Evie were finding conversation hard, then Jack and Ronnie were not speaking much either. Yet all this was while Ronnie and Evie had shot up the billing and Ronnie, thanks again to Jack, had even acquired a theatrical title that Jack himself (who would never be Sir Jack either) would never acquire.

And Lord Archibald and his teddy bear had no difficulty in talking to each other at all.

Jack and Ronnie went back some years. They'd met when doing their time in the army. Both had, quite separately, challenged the military authorities by putting down as their civilian occupations in Jack's case not 'song-and-dance man' but 'comedian' and in Ronnie's 'magician'. In neither case were they dishonest or—even in Jack's—joking.

The army might have found all kinds of ways to punish them for their facetiousness, or alternatively attached them to one of their troop-entertainment units. It did something in between. It didn't send them on endless muddy exercises, but, taking them to be delicate artistic creatures, consigned them to quasi-civilian drudgery. It became their duty, as Jack would put it later, to guard and defend at all costs the Royal Corps of Signals' filing system.

It was not so cruel of the army, which might, after all, have dispatched them to somewhere where they could have got shot. They actually had most weekends off. As Jack would describe it in the Walpole, embellishing for Evie some of the stages in Ronnie's life that Ronnie seemed not to have fleshed out himself, it was every weekday in Blandford—'in the green bosom of Dorset'—and every weekend up to town, to maintain, in one form or another, their show-business links.

'Never mind the Signals, Evie. We were the BEF. Back every Friday.'

During this period Jack became known for his ability to entertain the whole hut, before lights out, with vivid impersonations (he might have become a Lord Archibald) of almost any officer who'd come their way, and Ronnie became known as a man you played cards with at your peril. He might not only win, but suddenly turn the game into something else altogether.

After the army they'd kept up their connection and even become for a while an ill-fated double act. A comedian-cum-song-and-dance man *and* a magician? It was never going to work. But it was Jack who, some time after the amicable split and when he'd advanced considerably as a solo performer, had come to the aid of his friend's still-struggling career.

When he'd signed up to compere the Brighton show for a second season (quite a coup) and thus to have some influence with the management, he'd said to Ronnie, 'Get yourself an assistant and I could fix you up with a spot next summer.'

It was not necessary for Jack to say that by assistant he meant female assistant. It was not necessary for him to spell out that magic was a fine thing—what else was magic but magical?—but magic *and* glamour, now you were talking.

Ronnie hadn't disagreed. This was 1958. He was a magician, but he'd learnt some of the unenchanting truths of the entertainment business. This was a chance to jump at. But his other response was also realistic. Hire an assistant, let alone a glamorous assistant? What with? He was close to penniless.

But all this was not long before Eric Lawrence, formerly known as 'Lorenzo' (and often in Ronnie's mind as simply 'The Wizard'), suddenly died.


Jack and Evie had not crossed paths before, but they were two of a kind and might quickly have spotted this in each other. The three soon became pals. It was natural. Ronnie and Evie owed to Jack that they were there at all—even, it could be said, that they had become engaged. Thus Jack himself had woven a kind of magic.

He put it differently to Ronnie: 'I only said get an *assistant*.'

Jack was not the getting-engaged type, though if he didn't join Ronnie and Evie in the Walpole it would usually be because he was otherwise engaged with some girl. Sometimes the girl would join them. The girl would be only too aware of being up against the regular core of three and thus of her own incidental status, but as Evie put it once to Ronnie, 'At least she was having her turn.' These passing girls, since they all blended into one, began to be known by Ronnie and Evie as 'Flora'. Who is Flora this week? Their real names didn't seem much to signify.

The saloon bar of the Walpole was a known theatricals' haunt and Eddie Costello occasionally slipped in for a pint of Bass and a shufty.

As they sat in the Walpole, the eyes of the current Flora would now and then catch those of Evie, or vice versa. Or Evie might notice the girl looking at the engagement ring on her finger. The girl might be eighteen or nineteen. Evie was by this time a seasoned twenty-five, but she'd once, not so long ago, linked arms with a troupe of prancing young things—all of them proper little Floras. She would give the girl clinging so determinedly to Jack's arm a complicated smile.

Oh yes, put Ronnie down beside this friend of his, Jack Robbins, and which one would any foolish girl go for? If she was a foolish girl. But Ronnie had something, Evie knew it by now. And didn't they anyway just have something between them? Their act was becoming quite a success, and wasn't this its simple secret? They *had* something anyway. They were good together, they were a natural pair. You know this, you feel it. She liked to think that when they were on stage people could see this something they had. And look, there was even her engagement ring, glinting on her finger, to clinch it.

The girl would blink back at Evie's smile and, still gripping Jack's arm, bury her nose in her drink.

When Jack introduced their act, whether as first spot after the interval or in its later enhanced status, he would sometimes say, ever the soul of magnanimity, 'And now, boys and girls, I want you to meet the real Mr Magic. Not like me, eh?' And give the nutcracker grin.

Jack Robbins and Evie White were two of a kind and perhaps, in those days, of a quite numerous breed. Like her, Evie would discover, Jack had had a mother who'd wound him up from the earliest age, like a little toy, to go on stage.

It was an option. If you had nothing else, you had at least your own person, you might use it to perform and entertain. Mothers of a certain upbringing themselves seemed to know this and, especially if there was no father any longer available—here too Evie and Jack would discover they were similar—might be keen to pass this knowledge on.

Evie had had such a mother, who had coaxed her and coached her and taken her along to little cattle-market auditions. Evie would always remember her mother saying after these occasions, 'Life is unfair, my darling, always was, always will be,' but then saying, with a beaming smile, 'but don't you worry, my sweetheart, your turn will come.'

What was she to believe in: the unfairness or the turn that was coming? And what did 'turn' mean? It sounded temporary. It sounded like what she *did* anyway. Easy! She could get up and, without hesitation and almost by second nature, twirl and smile and do things with her arms and even, in the right shoes, click her little heels and toes, and open her mouth to sing. But so far none of the men and sometimes women who sat at the tables with their pencils had singled her out from all the other striving elbowing girls of eleven or twelve, all primed and tarted up by their mothers, who could do much the same. Or better. 'Next please!'

'You must look after your legs, Evie. But I think they can look after themselves. And you must keep smiling, never forget your smile. You have the legs and you have the looks, my angel, but I think it's your voice we must work on.'

It was true. She had the legs, they would only get longer and lovelier, and she had the looks and knew how to use them. She could smile, she could dance, but—life *is* unfair—she could never sing, no matter how much she opened her mouth and struggled to use it. So she would have to do things that wouldn't expose this deficiency.

Which wasn't in fact so difficult when she found herself at last locking arms with some of those other girls who'd once been eleven and twelve, high-kicking and wheeling and swaying this way and that with them—and always smiling, smiling! If they had to sing, well, she could let the others carry her while she mimed enthusiastically.

*Keep your sunny side—up—up!*

Evie White. Wasn't she just a chorus girl once? Wasn't she in some act once? In variety.

But Jack, who'd had the same sort of start in life and gone through the same early maternal training, could do all sorts of things and could sing too.

*There'll be no more sobbin' when he starts throbbin' ...*

Ronnie Deane was a different kettle of fish and as Evie, but only with some persistence, would find out, had had a different introduction to the world of entertainment, and a different kind of mother.

Once, when he was only five, Ronnie's mother had taken him, gripping his hand, round a few corners from where they lived to the gates of a school, where she believed he would learn things that would guarantee him a better life than either his put-upon mother or his father, who was not often to be seen, had achieved.

Those mornings, sometimes touched by a bracing frost, would seem later to Agnes Deane to have been some of the few bright interludes in her parental life.

'Be good, Ronnie, be a good boy,' she would say, with a final squeeze of his hand. A sound and well-meant instruction, and Ronnie was up for abiding by it. Soon he would be able to take himself, eagerly and proudly, to those once-feared school gates. But it would not be long before his mother, once again clutching his hand and still trying to assuage his fears (as well as her own), would have to take him to another place of depositing.

Agnes Deane. Life had not been fair and never would again. She lived with Ronnie and, if only occasionally, with Ronnie's father in the humblest of houses in Bethnal Green, but it was at least a house. It even had a tiny backyard that contained a necessary outhouse, an ever-diminishing heap of coal and, propped against the outhouse wall, a tin tub which was the only means of general ablution.

Ronnie's father was called Sid. Agnes's father was called Diego. Sid was a merchant seaman. Agnes was a charwoman. Though she was herself thoroughly English, even thoroughly East End, her Spanish descent was enough to have given her once for Sid a touch of exotic allure, and was enough to have given Ronnie his most noticeable features, his sleek black hair and penetrating dark eyes.

Since what happened with Agnes had happened in his own town, Sid was unable to escape his responsibilities in the traditional way of sailors. To his credit, though with some persuasion from Diego (Sid had once claimed that Diego intended to cut his throat), he'd shouldered these responsibilities by marrying Agnes and always returning, if after long absences, to her and his son. And he made sure that, even during his time at sea, a portion of his modest pay packet regularly reached his wife.

Thus Ronnie would remember his father as a mere visitor, a figure who might suddenly turn up, then just as suddenly be gone again. Almost because of their brevity, these periods of his father's presence could be indelibly vivid.

Once, Sid Deane had come home with a parrot, and with all the bluster of a man who thought that coming home with a parrot would be a very good idea. The parrot's name was Pablo, and it could even confirm it by saying so: 'Hello, I'm Pablo!' And Pablo was the Spanish form of Ronnie's middle name. So—this was an important but never clearly answered question for Ronnie—was the parrot essentially a father's gift to his son? Or was it a tribute to his mother's Spanish ancestry?

It was a beautiful bird, its feathers a brilliant mix of green and blue with flashes of red and on its throat a bib of glowing yellow. Even if it hadn't been able to tell you its name, could you ever forget such a creature?

Ronnie's mother did not like the parrot. It was not welcome in her house and no sooner had his father left again than, to Ronnie's consternation, she sold it to a pet dealer eager to acquire such a rarity.

This was not so long after Ronnie had started school, but he was present, one evening, when the man came to collect the parrot, cage and all. He watched when the man took curled-up notes from his pocket and gave them to his mother. He did not know how the price had been agreed, or the value of a parrot, and he did not know how to protest or intervene. He hadn't been taught about such things at school, yet he was conscious that he was getting a sharp lesson in the ways of the world at which he was miserably unproficient. His helplessness made a nothing of him.

Later, lying in bed, he was full of the most vehement reckonings. He would cease trying to be a good boy. His mother was not the woman he thought he knew. Who should he hate more, her or the pet man? He imagined a scene—though it was useless to imagine it now—in which he might have forestalled all this pain in a way that was perhaps just as painful, but might have been the only decent expedient. He might have seized some moment while his mother was out and opened the door of the cage, having first opened the window or back door. He might at least have offered Pablo his freedom and choice in the matter.

'Off you go, Pablo!'

He was barely six. These thoughts boiled up inside him, then boiled down again, but never entirely went away. And the moment had to come when his father next arrived home to find no parrot.

Ronnie wisely resolved that he would not say anything. It was up to his mother. It was the moment of truth.

Where was it then, Sid Deane had naturally enquired. Where was Pablo? In its brief residency the parrot had been capable, amazingly, of voicing both that question and its confident answer: 'Where's Pablo? Here I am!'

But now, to Ronnie's astonishment, his mother had a quick answer too: 'It flew away.'

This was a brazen lie, but, once more floored by events, Ronnie thought it best to maintain his silence—he was dumbstruck anyway—and did not say she had sold it to the pet man. Thus, in effect, he took his mother's side, and when his father had looked at him for corroboration he had stared sheepishly at his feet as if he might even have been the one to have let the bird escape. This, after all, had been his fantasy.

He was too young to think it through, but had he

adopted this pose more thoroughly and even turned his fantasy into a lie of his own, he might have self-sacrificingly reconciled his parents. Though how would that have helped him? His silence was self-sacrificing and painful enough.

In her defence Mrs Deane might have said that Sidney Deane had only left her with another mouth to feed. What did parrots eat? And it was a squawking mouth too.

When, much later, Evie asked Ronnie about his early years, she would get only certain things out of him. He was a secretive man, perhaps magicians need to be. Getting him to talk about his mother or father was not easy, and yet it had nothing, surely, to do with magic. She was happy to talk about her own parents—though there was not much to say about her father. She was even happy, when the time came, for her mother to meet Ronnie. He was her future husband, wasn't he?

But Ronnie was a cards-to-the-chest man. For example, Evie would never know anything, though it had made a formative and lasting impression on Ronnie, about the parrot. Yet in one sense whenever she looked at Ronnie she was looking straight at it. Pablo was Ronnie's stage name.

'Why Pablo, Ronnie?'

'It's my middle name, isn't it?'

It felt like only half an answer.

Even without the parrot as a bone of contention, those intervals when Ronnie's father was at home could be full of altercation, and not what they ought to have been—happy and domestically complete. They rarely passed without some explosive argument in which it would seem that though his mother might have been glad, even relieved that her husband had deigned to make one of his appearances, she might be even gladder when he left again.

After these outbursts she might sometimes collapse into tears or, more often, simply look as though she were breathing fire. And after them Sid might draw Ronnie aside and, as if to secure some understanding and solidarity with his son before he departed again, say philosophical things such as 'Spanish blood, Ronnie' or even 'Spanish passion', and generally imply that Ronnie should not make the same mistakes in life as he had.

Ronnie would come to miss his father, rarely seen as he was, and would try to soothe the pain of it through his own philosophical reflection that surely he could only miss his father in the same way that he missed the parrot: as one might miss an apparition and not a perma-nent fixture, as one might miss something that might not have been there in the first place. But then wasn't that true of everything?

And he missed the parrot.

One day in 1939 Agnes took the eight-year-old Ronnie to a railway station, knowing that she must part with him in a serious way, but not knowing that, except for one more snatched visit, she would never see her husband again. Nor, though in a different sense, would she ever see again, since he would have changed, the son she was now relinquishing.

He was still, when all was said, her good little boy, her only child, her pride and joy, and she said to him more than once again now, 'Be a good boy, Ronnie.' Though she knew this was not like taking him to school. His education, his future, was now entirely unknowable. But so was everyone's.

She had invested—and for Agnes such a thing was not a trivial purchase—in a new white cotton handkerchief which she'd tucked into her sleeve. Word had got around among the mothers that it might be a good item to bring, since it would assist in the act of waving and make them more visible to their departing children. Its other, more obvious purpose was not emphasised.

She hadn't had to do this thing, it was not compulsory, but a great national plan was afoot to remove children to places of safety, and what mother wouldn't want to do the safest thing for her child?

The moment came when the women had to remain behind the barrier, so they could only wave, while the children were herded and counted on the platform before being assigned their places on the train. They all wore labels and had gas masks in cardboard boxes round their necks, so that even before they departed they were already lost and indistinguishable in their general similarity and milling. Agnes could no longer pick out her son's head. At the same time the children could no longer pick out their own mothers among the press at the barrier. The flurry of handkerchiefs, like a frantic flock of white birds, only made it more difficult, as did—working in both directions—the blurring caused by tears. Some mothers didn't know which use to put their handkerchiefs to.

But Agnes, even though she could not discern Ronnie any more, kept waving while trying not to weep—even when the children were all packed onto the train and could not be seen anyway, even when the train clanked out of the station and disappeared.

When she could wave no more she returned across London (Paddington itself was quite a journey) to the sudden marooning emptiness of the house in Bethnal Green. How she missed her Ronnie. She hadn't had to part with him, yet she had. It was the best thing. This is what motherhood could sometimes mean: acts of dutiful resignation. She dried her tears. Her misery hardened, as it so often had before, into a sense of her own long-suffering fortitude.

Why should she weep if her Ronnie was safe? Now it would be her lot—and she didn't know the half of it yet—to endure air raids. She would have to scurry to shelters where she would cower with equally terrified neighbours while bombs fell, any one of which might reduce this home of hers to nothing or, if she was so unlucky, even obliterate herself (sometimes she might even wish one would). But at least her Ronnie, though far from her, would be well out of it.

She dried her eyes on the now-grubby handkerchief and made a vow: that she would not use it again, but nor would she wash it or fold it away. She would merely keep it as it was, with all this day's anguish still in it, until the war was over, like some charm. But she had no more use for tears.

Meanwhile Sid—and how like him—would be even further away and even more well out of it. Out there on the blue ocean. Safe as houses.

Ronnie, on his packed train, wept and snivelled a good deal. It was hard not to when so many around him were doing the same. It was now clear to all of them that this dreaded event was not a hoax or mere threat, but a cruel fact. Perhaps their lamenting was mixed with a surge of infant outrage. How could their mothers have possibly done this to them?

Perhaps at the same time the mothers had been visited by some chilling premonition of the hellish stage in its history the world was now reaching, such that their handkerchief-waving might have served another half-conscious function: an act of propitiatory surrender. Please can we have our children back? But it was too late.

Perhaps the children also had been touched by truths far beyond their actual situation. In any case, the more they were separated from their mothers by the clacking train, the more they wept for these women who had done this monstrous thing to them, the more they conjured up unbearably sweet images of them. Ronnie felt again the squeeze of his mother's hand as she'd left him, that first time, at the school gates. What terrible gates awaited him now?

Round his neck was the label declaring where he had come from and where he was being sent. And of course who he was. Though it seemed to Ronnie that during this period of his transportation, of this general harsh reshuffling of lives, even his identity had become uncertain.

He had no clear idea where he was going. 'Oxfordshire'. Where was that? And the address of his destination began not, like most addresses, with a number, but with a baffling name: 'Evergrene'. What did that tell him?

It was a long time before it struck him—words could have a way of slipping by you then suddenly speaking: Evergrene. It chimed softly with his own name, as it did with his place of birth. He didn't know whether this was an encouraging sign or a dark omen. As he inclined towards the latter, fear began to replace mere misery.

But it's remarkable how quickly, especially when you

are only eight, the whole mood and tilt of things, even the very nature of the world itself, can change.

This great exodus of children had many consequences, not all benign. There would be horror stories. Some went to dreadful encampments. Some went to so-called 'good homes' to be imprisoned, enslaved—worse. Some would even feel compelled to escape from their sanctuaries, slinking back, like aliens in their own country, to take their chances with the bombs.

But Ronnie was to arrive at a house in the depths of the countryside—he had never known countryside before—where, except for the blackout curtains and a few other minor privations and inconveniences, you might never have known that a war was going on. Evergrene.

He soon forgot about the war and quickly began to believe that this place he'd been sent to was where he really belonged, even that his previous life, including his home in Bethnal Green and the existence of his own parents, Agnes and Sid, must have been the result of some mix-up or misunderstanding.

In this house lived Mr and Mrs Lawrence, Eric and

Penelope, now in their middle years, with no children of their own. They had been only too willing to do their bit, in their charitable and non-combative way, by taking in this 'Ronnie'. But it seemed to Ronnie, almost from the start, that it might be him doing them the favour. He was like a gift they were gladly receiving. There was gratitude on their side too, not just the gratitude that he'd been told he ought to feel towards them.

'Remember to say thank you, Ronnie' had been among his mother's most fervent parting words, though clearly uttered between tight lips.

But he did feel gratitude, and rapidly overcame his determination not to express such a cowardly emotion. He soon began to wish, though he knew he was to be transplanted only 'for the duration', a once appalling phrase which he knew might mean years, that he could stay in Evergrene for ever. Though this would be like wishing (but Ronnie soon stopped thinking about this too) that the world's current bout of slaughter and destruction might never end.

Evergrene was unlike any house in his experience. For just two people it was enormous. It had separate rooms for doing different things in. It had a dining room for dining in. What was dining? It had a bathroom with a huge white tub in it. It had a sitting room—a *room* just for sitting in. It had two separate little rooms for shitting in.

Even the garden—garden!—which seemed to extend indefinitely till it merged into trees, had separate bits: a vegetable patch, a lawn, flower beds, a greenhouse and a cold frame. What was a cold frame? There was even an ancient, withered but clearly strong man called Ernie who came now and then to 'do' the garden. For a brief period Ronnie thought that Ernie lived in the greenhouse.

As if the house and garden were not enough, there was also a *car*. Thanks to petrol rationing, it was sparingly used, but Ronnie would get his chances to ride in it and would often sneak into its rickety wooden garage just to check it was real.

To all of this he had responded, in his first astonishment, with an unspoken expletive that he would never have used aloud in front of the Lawrences, nor indeed his own mother—he was only eight and still basically a good boy—yet it was proof, as was his accent and other things about him, that he'd known the rough life of the East End.

'Fucking 'ell,' Ronnie said to himself. 'Fucking 'ell.'

Here, anyway, Ronnie began his new (his proper?) life. Here he existed, while the world disintegrated, in security and comfort—in luxury, by any standard he had known.

More than this. Here he was fondly looked after and appreciated—the word really began to be 'loved'—by Mr and Mrs Lawrence, so that it gradually became a struggle to think of his mother, dodging bombs and thus to be pitied, in Bethnal Green. Where was Bethnal Green, and were bombs really dropping on it? Or to think of his father. Where was he? Where had he ever been?

It was part of Eric and Penelope's earnest commitment to their responsibilities that they strove not to supplant Ronnie's parents and to ensure he kept in touch with them. But this was difficult and in the case of Ronnie's father impossible. Agnes herself had once declared that 'out of touch' was Sidney Deane's middle name. For all the Lawrences' scrupulous efforts, Ronnie came to seem more and more like their own child.

Evergrene had a telephone. Ronnie's mother was encouraged to call at any time. It was vital anyway, when the air raids began, that they should all know she was safe. Ronnie was unable to convey to Mr and Mrs Lawrence what an extraordinary object a telephone would have been to his mother (it was for him too another of the exotic wonders he was now living with) and how the idea of speaking on such a thing to the occupants of Evergrene—even merely having to hear the well-spoken tones of Eric Lawrence— might have daunted her more than Hitler's bombs.

And perhaps Mr and Mrs Lawrence were also naive— though Ronnie could not have indicated this to them—in their impressions of conditions in London, including the state of repair of many a public telephone box.

Mr Lawrence, all in the cause of doing his bit, had signed up as an air-raid warden. He had a uniform and a helmet and every other night, alternating with another local warden, he went out into the dark to keep watch. Yet the truth was that even while London and other cities suffered, hardly a bomb fell in their part of the country. Ronnie would sometimes feel that Mr Lawrence's warden's uniform was a hoax—merely a costume he dressed up in. The whole thing seemed a bit of a fraud. And Eric Lawrence himself would retain from his time as a warden the principal memory of an uncanny nocturnal peace. While he patrolled, looking for offending chinks of light, he would gaze up at a sky (from which all hell was supposed to fall) that, because of the blackout, was lit by a spectacular display of stars.

He could grasp no better than Ronnie that whole swathes of London might be on fire.

Ronnie began to attend a local village school—Mrs Deane would not have to fear that her son's education was being neglected—and while he was there both Mr and Mrs Lawrence sometimes went into Oxford, again in the interests of doing their bit. When he was a little older he would come to understand that they served on 'committees' and were even part, in a small way, of the setting up of a thing called Oxfam, to help refugees. It came as something of a shock to be reminded that that was what *he* was, in a manner of speaking: a refugee.

Ronnie himself would get taken into Oxford—it wasn't so far—to be shown around. It was a special place. It had a thing called a university, and, what with his starting at the village school, Mr and Mrs Lawrence could now make the joke that Ronnie would always be able to say that he had 'been to Oxford', a joke which at first passed Ronnie by completely.

Oxford was certainly a special place, he had never seen anywhere like it, but what was particularly special about it, despite the sandbags round doorways and the soldiers drilling in college grounds, was that it would remain almost completely unscathed.

This too, during his early days as an evacuee, would make Ronnie think that the war must be some kind of fraud. Later, when he'd learnt other things that proved it was real, he learnt from Mr and Mrs Lawrence that there were factories not far from Oxford producing munitions. Yet still Oxford lay intact.

'Oh yes,' Mr Lawrence had said, 'I used to work in one of them myself, during the last war.' When he'd said it he'd given Penny Lawrence an odd smile, so that Ronnie had felt that some other hoax might be at work. But by this time he had acquired a quite developed sense that with Eric and Penny Lawrence anything might be the case.

All sorts of things began to emerge about them. Ronnie had never before had the opportunity to observe two grown-up people at close quarters, to see into their mysteries. It was perhaps that he'd grown up just sufficiently himself, and yet it was strange that the Lawrences could exert this fascination which he'd never felt with his own parents. His years as an evacuee were to give him many things, but almost from the start they gave him this curious sense of discovery and initiation.

It seemed that both the Lawrences had their 'business' to attend to in Oxford, and yet this was not their main or only occupation. It seemed that Eric Lawrence occasionally did work for other people—he was their 'accountant'. Penny Lawrence had once confided to Ronnie that Eric was very good at figures, at sums, yet she said it as if it was only one and not the most important of his interests. And then of course he had his nights going out as a warden. It seemed that they were people who might keep changing into a variety of roles and thus they were not like his own parents of whom Ronnie was only ever able to say, if required, that his father was a sailor and his mother was a char. As if that was what they had to be eternally.

It emerged that Penny Lawrence had once had a grandfather who'd lived in Evergrene, in this house, so that Penny had come here often when she was small—'When I was your age, Ronnie.' Then when her grandfather had died he'd left it to her—to her and Eric, since they were married by then—because she'd always loved being there as a child and he wanted her to have it.

'It was our windfall, Ronnie. Our blessing.' Ronnie didn't understand the meaning of either of these words, but he got the spirit of them and he kept the nice words— windfall, blessing—somewhere in the back of his mind.

Of course, Penny told him, her big brother Roy was miffed that she'd got the house—and lots of money besides—because she was her grandfather's favourite. But then—Penny gave a thin little laugh—Roy had gone off to Canada anyway and was doing very well out there thank you, so what did he need a house in Oxfordshire for? And Penny laughed again.

Ronnie understood very little of this—he knew nothing of Canada and what did he need to know about this Roy?—and yet Penny told him these things as if he were a grown-up himself and might have appreciated them. At the same time he realised that though he was supposed to think of them as Mr and Mrs Lawrence he had very quickly begun to call them in his head Eric and Penny, as if they were no different from friends he'd had at his school in Bethnal Green. And he quite soon felt, though it was not as if they ever formally said he could, that he might call them by these names aloud. Or rather that there were times, and he understood the difference between them very clearly, when he might say 'Mr Lawrence' and times when he might say 'Eric'.

When Mrs Lawrence, or Penny, had these little grown-up chats with him, even talking about her brother Roy, she would suddenly seem to remember that he was just a child and say, for example, 'But shall we have a game of snakes and ladders?'

There was a whole cupboard full of games. Games!

Or—much more interestingly—she might look at him with a sudden soft expression which Ronnie, to his surprise, could quite accurately interpret as her wishing he was hers, and which might melt even further into a look that almost seemed to say that he *was* hers—so her wish had come true. It was a quite wonderful look and it was quite wonderful to see the way it turned from one thing into another. And it was much better than any game of snakes and ladders.

These conversations—or games or looks—occurred when Mr Lawrence had to go into Oxford by himself. When Ronnie returned from school he and she would have an hour or so together. Their little chats (though Ronnie mainly listened) always seemed to reveal something new. For example, one day Penny said that Mr Lawrence would be staying all evening in Oxford and wouldn't be back till late. This was because he was giving a show. A *show*? Ronnie felt sure that Mrs Lawrence was teasing him and was daring him to ask, 'What kind of show?' And so he didn't say it, which would have been falling into some sort of trap.

Yet he enjoyed being teased and it seemed that Mrs Lawrence enjoyed teasing him. And it was true that Mr Lawrence didn't return till late that night and Ronnie, in his bedroom but woken by sounds below (the car being eased into the garage), distinctly heard Mrs Lawrence say, 'How did it go, darling?' And then Mr Lawrence say, 'Not bad.'

Such snippets of adult life were like nothing Ronnie had known before. They were like something you might see in a cinema, a place where he'd only ever been twice.

And yet everything might turn around. Penny Lawrence often wore a big floppy cardigan with large side pockets into which she would thrust her hands and waggle them, as if she was trying to sprout wings. Or just for the fun of waggling them. She was just like a girl. A girl! He could see how she must have done this same waggling thing when she was a child—done it in this very house in front of her grandfather and her stuck-up brother Roy—and had never got out of the habit.

Ronnie began to like Penny Lawrence very much—or he understood how Eric Lawrence might like her. And he liked Eric too. He would start to wonder, though quickly put a stop to this thought, what his mother might feel if she could see him and Penny Lawrence having their chats.

And he could never picture his mother as a girl.

Soon after his arrival at Evergrene a system of postcards had been instituted. His mother might write: 'All well here—Love Mum.' And Ronnie might write back: 'All well here—Love Ronnie.' These postcards, though he didn't know it, were not unlike numerous postcards servicemen would send home, which had to be short and sweet for reasons of censorship.

Ronnie would be encouraged by Mr Lawrence to say more, to describe his life at Evergrene, his visits to Oxford even, but Ronnie was inclined not to do this. He did not want his 'All wells' to betray anything more than just that—though he had been urged, with some coughing and embarrassment on their part, to state that Mr and Mrs Lawrence were 'very nice'. Which was true.

And how could he possibly convey to his mother such things as the fact that Eric and Penny sometimes had friends round, other grown-ups, for the evening—on the nights when Eric wasn't doing his warden duties (or giving a 'show'). Lying in bed, he could hear them talking and laughing. And once, before their evening started, they'd got him to come down, in his pyjamas, to be introduced or just displayed, and when he'd gone back up the stairs he'd plainly heard one of the visitors say, it was a woman's voice, 'What a charming little boy.' Then he heard Penny Lawrence say, 'Yes, he is.'

He'd never been called that before, never imagined that he might be called it. Charming.

But the most remarkable thing was that, though it was just Mr and Mrs Lawrence having a few friends round, they were all dressed up, the women in particular had nice dresses and necklaces and sparkly earrings and had done things to their hair (you couldn't have imagined Penny doing her waggling thing). It seemed to Ronnie that they'd all changed, that the women had become beautiful and the men handsome, that they were all charming—yes, that was really the word. Everyone was charming, they had drinks in their hands. Was this what was meant by putting on a show?

Over in one corner of the sitting room (as he'd learnt to call it) was a table that he'd never seen before. It was square and had a surface that was entirely bright green. On it were a couple of packs of playing cards, neatly stacked, but there was something else. A top hat. Yes, a top hat. Not an object that Ronnie was familiar with, but he was not mistaken. It was turned upside-down, brim uppermost, so you felt it might be being used as a container for all sorts of things.

Ronnie took in all of this, even as, briefly, he was being made an exhibit of himself. They all said goodnight to him and he managed to say goodnight to them, and the green of the table made him think of the name of this place he had come to and, though he was beginning to get used to it, the sheer astonishment of it all.

Things were not just all well at Evergrene, they were bloody fantastic. But to say this might (he was capable of perceiving it) hurt his mother, and it was not anyway in his interest to reveal that he was living the life of Riley. At the same time he strongly suspected that his mother's 'All wells' were not exactly truthful either. How could they be if bombs were really dropping on London? (Were they?) And he could well recall how she'd once said a parrot had flown away when in fact she'd sold it for clean profit.

The postcards served their function: they knew each other to be alive. Ronnie was aware that both Mr and Mrs Lawrence themselves wrote to his mother and he couldn't control what they said. Perhaps they were reporting on him. He knew anyway that for a while they'd had the idea that Mrs Deane might like to come and visit her son, might even like to stay. Might even like to stay *for the duration*. Wouldn't that indeed be the best solution to everything?

These suggestions caused a cloud to hover temporarily over Ronnie's generally euphoric existence and he'd felt a great relief when they were not taken up. It became gradually clear that his mother had seldom replied to Mr and Mrs Lawrence's letters and never at any length. They wondered why.

Ronnie realised that though he was only a small boy he was in some things more versed than his vastly older hosts.

After a while the postcards were exchanged less frequently. An acceptance grew—was even allowed to blossom—that Evergrene was Ronnie's home now. He was happy in it (he was happier than he'd ever been) and the Lawrences were happy to have him. Their loving-kindness enveloped him and they'd been diligent in testing its possible limits. Now it might simply prevail.

Wasn't *this* the best solution of all? Even if one might fairly ask how could any of it be? How could you have had one life and then simply exchange it for another?

One instance of the loving-kindness Ronnie would never forget. In all this dizzying uncertainty as to who his effective parents were, it fell to the Lawrences to tell Ronnie that his real, his true yet so often unseen father was—no more.

How this news had been passed on to Eric and Penelope Ronnie would never know, but the couple clearly understood that they must be the breakers of the news and that, with no experience of raising a child yet with all their years, they must take on whatever this might entail.

They were surprised at Ronnie's lack of response, his muteness, his containment, as if this thing might have had nothing to do with him or as if he had simply not registered it at all. It was all just shock perhaps.

Perhaps, and this might be their own fault, the poor boy simply didn't know what to believe.

His father had been 'lost at sea'. He was 'missing'. These were the official phrases that conveyed yet muddled the truth. The Lawrences had wished, for considered reasons, to avoid any more definite words. So had any of it sunk in? Which was an unfortunate way even of framing the question.

It was only when that evening Eric Lawrence went to tuck Ronnie in and see if he was all right, that emotion suddenly spilled—surprising even Ronnie himself with its flow and force. Mr Lawrence had thought of Ronnie lying alone, having to make his own voyage through the night while understanding (perhaps) that his father would never voyage again. Perhaps he wouldn't be able to sleep.

Mr Lawrence had gone up and sat on the edge of Ronnie's bed. Ronnie might have said, in one of those never-written letters, that it was a very nice comfortable bed with a pale-green bedspread, in a very nice big bedroom with curtains matching the bedspread, though they now took second place to the familiar blackout curtain. The window overlooked a huge garden.

Ronnie had never communicated any of these things to his mother and Mr Lawrence for his own part had no notion of the pokiness of the sleeping accommodation in Bethnal Green. But he'd wondered if Ronnie, apart from thinking of his father, had also been thinking of his mother and whether she too (this was October 1940 and the Blitz was in full swing) was able to get to sleep.

He put his hand on Ronnie's forehead, cupping its smallness with his palm. It was a spontaneous gesture not intended, perhaps, to be fatherly and more like the action of a doctor feeling for a fever, but Ronnie realised that his own father had never done anything so tender, even though he might have been capable of it.

The hand on his brow had a strange tingling power.

'You must go to sleep, Ronnie. It is the best thing. Just to sleep.'

Ronnie had almost at once felt his eyes droop, but

Mr Lawrence had added, 'I think perhaps that's how you should think of it. That he is sleeping too, among the fishes.'

It was these words, the idea that both he and his father might just be sleeping, or it was the vision of lots of glittering fish, but there had sprung from Ronnie—though it was only when Mr Lawrence had kissed his forehead and crept out—a sudden convulsive upwelling of tears. He could not stop them, they went on and on, enveloping him till he fell asleep. So that his last thought perhaps was that his own tears were like the deep salt water, if only a tiny part of it, under which his father lay slumbering and submerged.

Why had he cried? For his father certainly, but also for some great swamping confusion—confusing yet kind. For this extraordinary metamorphosis that had occurred in his life. For the boy, weeping before on a train, who'd not known any of this was to come—who'd cried then for his mother, for whom he was not crying now. From guilt and dismay that he could cry now for his father yet feel that he had another already to replace him. From drowning gratitude that he'd been taken and dropped down in so much goodness.

But more than this. More than all this bewildering

bounty. He had discovered by now his purpose in life. He had discovered, or it had been revealed to him, that Mr Lawrence was not just the owner with his wife of an enchanted place called Evergrene, but, though currently forced to work in a limited way (there was a war on: 'There isn't much call, Ronnie'), he was an accomplished magician.

One day Ronnie sat with Eric Lawrence on the low brick wall of the cold frame. He knew by now what a cold frame was, but one of its incidental functions was to serve as a convenient place to sit on warm days. Mr Lawrence, while they sat, was enjoying a mug of tea and Ronnie was enjoying a glass of ginger beer. The ginger beer was made by the Lawrences themselves—was there no end to the amazements of this place? The recipe had been given them, he was told, by Ernie, who seemed to have talents beyond gardening and who today was nowhere to be seen. Ronnie was now used to this. Sometimes Ernie was there, sometimes he wasn't.

Mrs Lawrence, after bringing out the drinks, had made herself scarce, as if aware that there was to be some man-to-man talk. Mrs Lawrence had a very nice way of saying whenever she proffered something, or sometimes for no clear reason at all, 'Here we are!' And Ronnie had come to love this bright and strangely echoing phrase. Here we are! How happy. And true.

And Eric Lawrence did indeed have something special to impart.

After sipping some tea he smacked his lips and looked around.

'The great trouble with this garden, Ronnie, is the rabbits. They come and they eat everything.'

This was a strange remark because though the garden backed onto fields and woods Ronnie had never seen any rabbits in it. Perhaps he hadn't been looking. Perhaps they were something else that Ernie dealt with. They had more than once eaten rabbit pie—something Ronnie had never eaten in Bethnal Green, but which in the country seemed to be a wartime staple.

Mrs Lawrence had once said, when serving it, 'What would we do without Ernie?' She'd looked very fondly at Ronnie while putting a serving of pie on his plate, so that he'd almost thought she'd said, 'What would we do without Ronnie?' It was a pleasing mistake, as was the idea that he and Ernie might have changed places. If he'd been an older and more polished being, Ronnie might have said to Mrs Lawrence, 'Ah—but what would we do without your wonderful cooking?' And Mrs Lawrence might have felt a catch in her throat.

But he'd never seen any rabbits in the garden.

After his emphatic complaint about the invading rabbits, Mr Lawrence suddenly said, 'Well bless me!' He would use such cosy expressions—they were a bit like Mrs Lawrence's 'Here we are!'s. They made Ronnie feel all the more alert about his inner 'Fucking 'ell's.

'Bless me,' Mr Lawrence said, 'there are some of the devils right now.'

Ronnie looked this way and that—the vegetable patch, the lawn—but he couldn't see a single rabbit.

'No, Ronnie. I mean the ones behind you.'

Ronnie turned and there, within the low brick confines of the cold frame and beneath its half-raised glass panels, were one, two, three—no, four rabbits. And each one of them was pure white. It looked as if there had been a remarkable and remarkably localised snowfall. But the snow was alive.

They had not been there before. They really had not been there just before. They seemed not at all shy, happily munching at some just-shooting lettuces.

'You see what I mean,' Mr Lawrence nonchalantly said. Then he said abruptly, 'But what was that?' and pointed at something seemingly in mid-air. Ronnie could not help but be drawn to his straightened finger.

'Look again, Ronnie. Turn around.'

The rabbits were gone.

It was the beginning. Even perhaps—after more than one start already—the true start of his life.

'Would you like to know how that was done, Ronnie? Would you like to know how that happened?' He had taken a quick sip of his tea. 'One step at a time of course.'

So it was that Ronnie began what Jack Robbins would call his 'sorcerer's apprenticeship'. So it was that years later, having pursued with dogged and solitary determination but with no great profit what he would sometimes speak of as his 'calling', Ronnie put an advert, following Jack's advice, in one or two appropriate places.

'Magician's Assistant Wanted. Suit Young Lady. Previous Stage Experience Essential.'

And Evie White had answered it.

In the many years in between, Ronnie had become,

thanks to Mr Lawrence's exclusive instruction, a promising and competent magician, but Mr Lawrence had stressed that it was a long and not necessarily lucrative road, and was Ronnie sure? (Ronnie was certain.)

Mr Lawrence's tutelage could not last for ever. It was governed by the course of the war. This applied to other things even more exercising than magic. As the war drew to its close Ronnie felt a new qualm enter his life, the reverse of and more complicated than the one he'd felt when his mother had taken him to Paddington and to an unknown fate.

He was fourteen now, a big boy. Was he still a good one? The Lawrences would have said that he was. Was he a changed and even improved one? Yes. Setting aside that he had learnt how to perform magic—something his mother had no knowledge of and couldn't possibly have imagined—his time at Evergrene had been an education. He had attended more than one local school and had learnt things, not just magic, directly from Mr and Mrs Lawrence, educated people themselves. Another wonder of the house was that it was sprinkled with books.

But Ronnie had picked up from the air at Evergrene, from his very habitation of it, a sense of things, a taste for things that he knew—he still had memories that enabled him to know—were going to seem distressingly foreign when he returned to London. Yet this would be just his side of it.

He could at least begin to see it, though he did not want to, from his mother's point of view. She might scoffingly say he'd 'gone up in the world', he'd 'got ideas about himself'—she who'd taken him to school, assuring him it would lead to a better life. She might feel only humiliated by these other loftier parents who'd taken over. Under the guise of being a deserving case for protection (though it had been *her* decision), he had, in effect, deserted her.

Moreover, she was a widow now. She had survived bombs, she had trembled in shelters. He had known not merely shelter, but—she didn't yet know it—a privileged, even a charmed existence.

Such thoughts began to gnaw at him. As the war seemed to be ending he was guilty again of wanting it to go on, or of hoping for some other way of prolonging his time at Evergrene, so that the issue of his mother would not have to be faced.

Mr and Mrs Lawrence too secretly wished that his stay with them might continue, would have arranged it if they could. They had got used to him, their little Ronnie—though he was no longer so little. They were about to be bereaved.

Even the availability of magic, it seemed, could not solve everything. It could bring about extraordinary transformations, but not alter the fundamentals of life. It was a lesson a budding magician would be wise to heed. Perhaps Mr Lawrence had tried to instil it. Or perhaps he was too afraid himself of waking up from this dream of having a child—a protégé, a pupil. Or of dashing Ronnie's own fledgling ambitions.

On a June day in 1945 Ronnie Deane boarded a train at Oxford, a city still remarkably untouched, to go to a city of rubble. And now it was Mr and Mrs Lawrence who tearfully waved goodbye.

Ronnie returned to a London transformed—what on earth had been going on?—and to a mother, it seemed to him, damaged and altered too, not beaten or even essentially changed, but hardened.

And after nearly six years how did he look to her? Improved, enhanced? Softened? Perhaps even a little soft in the head?

She was not going to stand for any nonsense anyway. He was nearly fifteen now and, since events had interrupted his education, was in the unfortunate position, while possessing no qualifications, of needing to earn a living. So what was he going to do about it?

Ronnie had his innocent answer and, cosseted by so much time away from the big city, he naively let out his secret.

'A magician, Ronnie? A magician! Please tell me you're having me on! Please tell me you're joking!'

His mother's language and manner became even harsher. In her head was the thought: Jesus Christ, it had been bad enough being married to a sailor. And Ronnie must have read her mind, since he had the sudden realisation: was he not now like his father, back from a long and absconding voyage?

'Jesus Christ, Ronnie! Jesus Christ!'

Then his mother had said something he'd never heard cross her lips and that would never have crossed his own in front of her, though he'd many times said it to himself, even in polite company.

'Fucking hell, Ronnie! Magic! Whatever fucking next?'

Oh he was back home all right, he was back in London, and what a welcome he was getting.

Having exploded, his mother had soon erupted into tears. It was a familiar cycle. But she wasn't asking to be comforted. It was another form of venting. Hardened? Like a stone, even when undergoing a wetting. And Ronnie might have burst into tears himself, but he was coming up to fifteen and couldn't.

But more than all this. More than this initial cutting down to size. The little house in Bethnal Green—how little it seemed—enclosed him like a prison. It was mostly unchanged and it was unscathed (other houses along the street were not there any more), and its humble endurance, like his mother's, might have spoken to him. But it was like a confinement. He felt guilty—why shouldn't he, returning to a prison cell? It had once housed his tiniest self. It had once briefly housed a parrot, which, according to his blatantly lying mother, had flown away. But how right she was now to be aggrieved.

And how he identified with that caged bird.

There followed a year or so in which mother and son attempted, somehow, to live with each other. The unbudging truth was that they did not know each other. Or it was more—Ronnie had to accept this—that Mrs Deane didn't know her son. *She* hadn't moved, *she* hadn't gone anywhere. She was still a charwoman. He pined for the Lawrences and all that he had now been separated from. She didn't understand, and wouldn't have sympathised if she had. And yet she knew he had found another home, another, better life. She felt shamed and wounded.

He acknowledged all this. He had done it to her. But he had been only one of the blameless objects (and fortunately not a victim) of a great historical emergency. He felt—it was a terrible thing to admit to himself—a stranger to his own mother. They did not know each other? They did not own each other. They even disowned each other.

There followed another period in which Ronnie 'left home' again, though he was never far from Bethnal Green and sometimes miserably slunk back again—he needed a bed somewhere. Might he have stolen back to the Lawrences, and might they have received him? With difficulty, yet with joy—yes.

But Ronnie knew—he turned sixteen, then seventeen—that he had to stand on his own feet.

This was an itinerant period, so different from any previously in his life, when he scraped a living somehow or other in theatres, doing whatever menial work there might be for him to do for a pittance, learning how they worked. Sometimes even revealing that he could do things himself—on stage, that is—and so starting to learn what a stage is like, what it asks of you, what a hard thing a stage can sometimes be. Learning also the ins and outs of that encompassing entity, 'the stage', its intricate and precarious webs of connection. Living, sleeping wherever he could, in some strange places, and—oh, he was growing up—with any girl who might have him and help him. Or sometimes vice versa. Any girl, and there were not a few of them, in the same rough, glittery, hopeful, deluded, stage-struck, thankless, magical business.

Eric Lawrence had said it would be tough. Was Ronnie ready? He'd said, and had smiled at his own doubletalk, 'There are no magic wands, Ronnie. There are magic wands, but there are no magic wands. Do you understand me?' Eric Lawrence had said it would take time and determination and had urged upon Ronnie that, though he had acquired now some of the basics of magic, there was something else he had to learn, and that was that he would be in the trade of entertainment.

Magic and entertainment were not always the same thing, but they had to combine if he was seriously to follow his vocation. And entertainment meant having to give the people what they wanted and not necessarily what he wanted and might be capable of doing. It meant understanding and bowing ('In every sense, Ronnie') to the audience. And it meant, above all, knowing about that thing called 'the stage'. This was something he could not teach at Evergrene.

So Ronnie had had to find out for himself.

But Eric Lawrence had added, not to make Ronnie too downhearted at all these harsh admonitions, 'And you will need a stage name. When you are on stage you will need a name—just as I was Lorenzo. What name do you think you should have?'

He had left only the slightest pause for Ronnie (who was anyway at a loss) to answer this question, as if asking it had been merely perfunctory.

'I think you should be called Pablo, don't you? Don't you think Pablo would be a good name for you?'

How had he *known*? But *had* he known? Ronnie had never mentioned the parrot. Even when his father had died—for some reason even more resolutely then—he had never mentioned the parrot, which must still have been in a cage somewhere, with some new owner, or some new pet dealer (how did pet dealers fare in a war?). Or even, if it had ever managed truly to fly away, in some place known only to itself.

'Where's Pablo? Here I am!'

Or perhaps—but Ronnie didn't want to think about this—perhaps it had been killed, a victim of the hostilities. Perhaps a parrot in a cage would be one of the first things to suffer, even to be brutally sacrificed, when bombs were otherwise whistling down on human beings.

But of course Eric Lawrence had another reason.

'It's your middle name, isn't it, Ronnie? It's your real name. Paul. Just like my real name was always Lawrence. I went for Lorenzo. But I think Pablo sounds rather better, don't you?'

And could he have got anywhere by calling himself just Ronnie?

Then anyway the army caught up with him and he had to go away and do his time. Never mind Pablo or any other name, he was now plain Private Deane, with a number. As luck would have it, he managed to get through it all doing something conveniently unsoldierly, but certainly not magical.

And at least it all vaguely placated his mother. He was doing a 'proper job' at last, with regular pay attached to it, some of which he duly sent her. And perhaps a year and a half in the army would knock all that magic rubbish out of him and show him what was what.

As it turned out, he could even get the train up to London at weekends and go to see her. Thanks to the army, his life had never been more ordinary. The army was even teaching him, in readiness for the great normalities of life, how to be a good little office boy. But he kept quiet with his mother about his actual military duties ('Oh, you know, marching up and down') and never told her (or even Jack that much) about the weekends he spent with the Lawrences. He would take a different train. There was a handy connection from Bournemouth.

My, my—Private Deane. How their little Ronnie had grown. All through the war he'd lived here and now here he was, a soldier himself. He sat down again on the wall of the cold frame. There was still ginger beer. Did soldiers drink ginger beer? Mrs Lawrence, perhaps having asked herself this question, had produced a bottle of White Shield. How had she known it had become his favoured tipple? He would even drink it in the Walpole.

He told his mother that these were weekends when he had to go for special training. It wasn't a lie. 'Training' was a useful word. To himself he might have used the phrase 'refresher courses'.

And it was in the army that he met Jack Robbins, later to be known as Jack Robinson, and most of those free weekends were mainly spent in Jack's company in London, getting up to business of one kind or another. Some of it was monkey business, but some of it really was useful business. Should he have introduced Jack to his mother? Would Jack have charmed her and convinced her of the multiple merits of a career in entertainment?

Or would even Jack have found her a hard audience to crack? Ronnie never met Jack's mother either. It was not what soldiers tended to do on leave, meet each other's mothers.

They teamed up as a double act, short-lived and doomed. 'Jack and Pablo'? No. 'Pablo and Jack'? No. 'The Two Amigos'? Yes, but not for long. It was a wise and friendly parting.

More wandering in the West End wilderness and in provincial dead-ends, while Jack progressed, even turning into 'Jack Robinson' and finding success, even one day telling his old friend—and amigo—that if he got an assistant . . .

Easily said, and perhaps something he might have told himself. There was just one small problem.

But then Eric Lawrence had died. The Lawrences were not so old, but nor were they spring chickens. Eric Lawrence had sometimes referred—it was another reason for his abandoning the stage—to his 'dicky ticker'. It was a blow, a sudden great gap in his world and a great clarification—magicians do die—and while having to hide his secret grief from his mother, Ronnie had gone specially, hiding this too, to see Penny Lawrence, to comfort her and to be at the funeral. He thought of the night when he had learnt that his father had died and of how Eric Lawrence had come in to comfort him and then slipped out again. How he'd found himself suddenly immersed in tears.

Evie White answered the advert.

And so she had walked like a gift (though she had no intention of offering any services for free) into the life of Ronnie Deane, just as Ronnie had once walked like a gift into the life of Eric and Penelope Lawrence. But Evie didn't know about all that then, she didn't know yet about the 'sorcerer's apprenticeship', which was anyway only Jack's mischievous phrase.

The man before her was slightly built and not imposing

though he had a head of smooth black hair and remarkable dark eyes. He had something about him that definitely grew on you.

He said, 'I've come into a little windfall, Miss White.'

Which was reassuring and interesting—both that he had such a thing and that he'd said it so soon after their saying their hellos. He hadn't needed to say it. She didn't need to know how he would pay her, so long as he did.

And she didn't need to know the nature of the windfall and wouldn't at that point have been so forward as to ask, though she was curious. She didn't know then, though she would gradually learn these things, that Eric Lawrence had died or that he'd been known as Lorenzo, or that in his will he'd left (with his wife's agreement) quite a tidy sum to Ronnie Deane, along with a good deal of his professional bits and pieces. That he was the sorcerer to whom Ronnie had become the apprentice.

'Windfall', she would think later, was a bit like saying 'sorcerer'. It was a hocus-pocus sort of word that might mean anything. Anyone could say they'd had a windfall. And if you were a magician perhaps you could whisk one up at any time.

It was the magic bit in the advert—anyone could be an 'assistant'—that had intrigued her and tempted her and why she was here on this October day. The idea of being involved in magic. Why not? She'd try anything once.

Though this man didn't look all that magical, and she wasn't entirely sure about the windfall. His saying in a modest way that it was 'a little windfall' could suggest that in fact it was not so little, but his saying it at all suggested that normally he might be on his uppers, which was a little like how things looked. Had he got his hands on this windfall yet?

But then, she was on her uppers too. It was another reason why she was here.

She smiled. 'I'm very pleased to hear that, Mr Deane.'

She crossed her legs. Keep smiling, Evie, and look after your legs.

'Suit Young Lady. Previous Stage Experience Essential.' What girl—or young lady—would answer such an ad? Not many, it seemed. She was here alone. But she had those two stated qualifications. And it seemed that singing wouldn't be involved.

It was a dusty rehearsal room upstairs behind the old Belmont Theatre. And was it an interview or an audition? Just the former it seemed.

'And it's Evie,' she said. 'You can call me Evie.'

From somewhere below there was the sound of stage

carpenters banging. She was used to such places. They hired them out by the hour when not needed by the resident company. It seemed clear he had no office or respectable place of residence. And what girl would have gone along to some grubby bedsit or flat? The studio with the noise of carpenters felt neutrally safe. On the other hand, she was alone. There was no little line of other hopefuls waiting on the stairs, and none was to materialise. No competition then?

'Tea?' he said. 'I'm having one myself. Milk? Sugar?'

Hardly magic words, but those dark eyes had something. She thought it best to accept.

He went off to some cubbyhole on the landing. If she'd got cold feet and felt like flitting that would have been her chance. He might have walked back in holding the tea only to find her gone, a disappearing act that might have impressed him, but not got her the job.

And her life might have been completely different.

'It's Ronnie,' he said. 'Please call me Ronnie. Here we are. Two mugs of char.'

Char? He was friendly anyway, he didn't have airs.

'I do a lot of my rehearsing here. I keep a lot of my gear here.'

Gear?

'I used to do a spot in one of their shows. They've been good to me.'

It was a bare, sky-lit room. Some chairs, a table at which they now sat, a low wooden platform which served as a stage. Anywhere less ready for magic would have been hard to find.

'Of course, all the rehearsing so far has been for my solo act. I've never worked with an assistant before.'

Ah.

He had seemed to pause over the word 'assistant' as if he should have come up with a better one, but now at least they were getting down to business. This was her opportunity to ask a question or two. And what would she be required to do?

'Regular magic stuff,' he said, unhelpfully. What on earth was 'regular magic stuff'?

'Stuff the public want. You have to give the public what they want and expect.'

This was a lesson she'd well learnt herself, though it was not really why she was here. There was something appealing about his slightly weary confidingness. But then was magic ever what people expected?

'I'll need to work out the material. But I'm always working on new illusions.'

Illusions?

He lifted his mug with a half-toasting gesture. 'We'll work it out together.'

Was that saying she'd got the job? It was certainly saying something. Work it out together. Over the rim of his mug, his eyes were particularly strong. The upper half of his face was the striking part. He seemed an unassuming and vague man in some ways, and on the underfed side. Perhaps to be a magician you had to be a bit dreamy. Yet in other ways he seemed quite sure of himself and he moved—she'd noticed it even as he walked in bearing the tea—with a certain poise. And the eyes were actually quite mesmerising.

The question, she realised, might have been not what did he want her to do, but what did he want to do with her?

He was sizing her up, she could tell. Fair enough. She was used to it. She was under no 'illusions' herself. She supposed that the principal role of a magician's assistant might be adornment. But she already felt an infectious sense of participation, of partnership in whatever it was they might do *together*.

And wasn't she sizing him up too?

'It will be a new departure for me as well, Ronnie.'

She was rather pleased with her sudden impressive turn of phrase: 'new departure'. Where had that come from?

But wasn't there anything he wanted her to do now? Interview or audition? It was a rehearsal room, after all. She couldn't of course perform any magic, but, for what it was worth, she might get up and show him what she *could* do. There had been no talk of bringing a costume, but she might hitch up her skirt and do a few turns and kicks, and that might clinch things, if they needed clinching. That might do the trick.

Had he even thought about a costume? She was going to need one, wasn't she? But there we are: she was already, in her head, getting in a huddle with him, even taking a coaxing lead. It was quite exciting. If the question of a costume was to come up, then she could easily supply one. Though should it be up to her? But any chorus girl worth her salt knew how to get, borrow, steal or simply possess a costume.

And when the moment did come, when he saw it—or rather saw her in it (and she could put on a show)—you could tell he thought his lucky day had really arrived. First a windfall, then this. Ding!

Magic? She couldn't do it herself? And why, when you thought about it, hadn't every man come up with the same simple crafty idea? 'Magician's Assistant Wanted.' When, later, she was on stage with Ronnie—performing, doing magic—she wasn't so unassuming herself as not to guess that every man in the audience was looking more at her than at him. Yes, the tricks were good, but she was the best trick of the lot. Or alternatively that they were thinking, of Ronnie: Wish I had his magic.

And of course if they were looking at her, they wouldn't be looking at the cunning things Ronnie was doing. It served a function. It was called, he would tell her one day, as if it were one of the most obvious and tedious principles of magic, 'diverting attention'. In the same apologetic way he would talk about 'the power of suggestion'.

He didn't ask her, that October day, to do anything. It was just the 'interview'—such as it was. And the tea. A bare, dusty, chilly rehearsal room on an autumn morning. But how oddly cosy and purposeful it became. Was this some little spell he had cast? They clasped their mugs of tea like workmen round a brazier.

'All in good time,' he said. 'Why don't we meet here next week? Tuesday? I can book us two hours on a Tuesday. We can get to work.'

So—she had got the job then? He had that unhurried

way of men who'd spent a lot of time avoiding things, dodging things—not volunteering for them—in the army. You could spot it. They were a breed. He couldn't yet be thirty, not much older than her. And she wondered how that might have worked: a magician in the army. It was hard to imagine this man being a soldier. But then it was quite hard to imagine him being a magician.

Should she have asked him to do a trick, just to test him?

Finally, as if he might have forgotten—she had coughed a bit and it was clear he'd never employed anyone before— he got round to the subject of what he would pay her. It was more than she'd expected. But she pretended it wasn't, and accepted.

He said, 'If we can work up an act over the winter, I know someone who might get us a slot in the Brighton season next summer.'

Everyone knows someone who knows someone. Everyone has a friend. It was something else she had learnt.

'By the way,' he said, 'my stage name is Pablo.'

She might almost have laughed. It was quite a switch, from Ronnie to Pablo, but he said it without a flicker of awkwardness, even, she felt, with a touch of pride. And Ronnie, it was true, was not a good stage name. And 'Pablo'—it went with the dark hair and those eyes, and that unexpected poise.

'And I think you should be "Eve".' There was not a hint of hesitation here either. 'Evie just doesn't work, does it? Eve. Pablo and Eve.'

And he was right. Evie was the same as Ronnie. And Pablo and Eve, yes, it had a certain ring.

It can't have been on that first Tuesday or even the second one, it must have been some other time, but it was in that rehearsal room anyway that she found herself saying, 'Ronnie, has anyone ever told you that you have smashing eyes?' It was bold and forward of her even then. But she was Evie White, who'd never been slow in coming forward and would give anything a go at least once.

It was in one of their tea breaks. It was all rather odd. One moment they were doing magic—they really were—next, they were stopping for tea. She sometimes made it herself now, they took it in turns. And it must have looked very odd too, a woman sometimes in little more than sequins and plumes in that cubbyhole, with its stained and smelly sink, filling the kettle, warming the pot. Her plumes could get in the way and upset things if she wasn't careful, but she'd learnt long ago to be aware of her attachments as an animal must be aware of its tail. Every chorus girl had this sixth sense.

Working with Ronnie was fun. She'd never thought magic might involve laughter, and perhaps Ronnie had never really thought it either. When performing, he could adopt the most serious, even scary expressions, she'd discovered, he could really change, but they would laugh a lot in their breaks. He was a magician and yet he could find all sorts of ordinary things strange or funny.

He began to say, now and then, about this or that, 'Fucking 'ell, Evie, fucking 'ell.' She didn't mind. If you don't like language then don't work in the theatre. She even felt slightly privileged. She felt he might have wanted to say it when he first saw her in her costume. 'Fucking 'ell, Evie.' And there was something oddly innocent about it. It was not so different from her mother saying, as she did about all kinds of things, 'Ooo-er!'

Was it when they were both blowing the steam off their mugs? No doubt she would have been using her own eyes too. He had got quite used to her now being around him in her costume. To having to allow for the feathers himself. There was a blanket she draped round herself, more practical than a dressing gown. It was like being a horse.

'Has anyone ever told you, Ronnie, that you have smashing eyes?'

Well, *she* had now. And anyway he gave his answer. Had she been asking for it—or for some answer with similar effect? And was she complaining?

'It's not the eyes, Evie, it's what they're looking at.'

And they didn't blink at all. Hers might have fluttered a bit.

His friend, his 'someone' who might give them work, was Jack Robbins, stage name Jack Robinson. He'd been slow in getting round to saying that.

But he wasn't slow in getting round to other things. When he first took her to meet Jack (who'd been away on tour up north) she wasn't of course wearing her costume, but she was wearing something else that was special. And perhaps both these precautions were just as well. If she were a man with a friend like Jack Robbins she too might have been slow in making the introductions, or at least wanted to take out some insurance first.

'Pablo and Eve'. Yes, it had a ring to it. And now she was wearing a ring. Ronnie had only just presented it to her, and it cemented the notion that though they were Pablo and Eve they were also Ronnie and Evie. She supposed he must have bought the ring with that windfall money as well, but that was not the right way to think about it.

An engagement ring with a little diamond bright as a star.

Now Evie White is seventy-five. It's 2009, not 1959 when she first wore that engagement ring. Fifty years! She looks at her face in a mirror.

The idea was that if they got the Brighton season—and they did—then they'd get married that September, when the show closed and they had the breathing space. They'd take a honeymoon and generally take stock—of Pablo and Eve, that is, not of Ronnie and Evie, though weren't they the same?

It's September now, 8th September. Almost exactly fifty years. And it's exactly a year since something else happened, in this very bedroom. Evie is sitting in it now. And suppose Ronnie could see her. Perhaps he can. Through the window the late afternoon light, deep gold, is starting to fade. She can see the yellowing leaves of the crab-apple tree in the garden.

She has taken off her pearls. It has been a taxing day. She might take off her face. She thinks she might just take off everything, though it's not so long since she put it all on, and lie down for a nap in the bed behind her.

Already a whole year, but it seems, today, like only yesterday. For a whole year now it has been the only constant fact, and not all the unchanged familiarity of this house and all its stubborn denials—framed photos of Jack everywhere, his jackets, his coats still hanging where he last put them—can make the fact any less of a fact or make it any more bearable.

And has she kissed the photos? And has she thrust her face into the jackets and coats, and even—? Of course she has.

Exactly one year ago, and the house is no less full of goneness. That's the word she still likes to use in her head: gone. Not dead. Not death. She had never liked to use those uncompromising words of Ronnie either. Just gone. 'Gone' implied it might be only temporary, or even—and even quite believably in Ronnie's case—an illusion, a word, she recalled, that Ronnie had always been keen on.

And not all the remembered voices that had once filled this house—the parties! the evenings!—can make its silence now any less crushing.

Once her mother had said to her that life was unfair, but her turn would come. And look what a turn it had turned out to be. Fifty years with Jack Robbins. Or not quite. Forty-nine. How unfair. But now, anyway, here she was, sitting pretty in Albany Square, guardian, curator and beneficiary of her late husband's shining career.

If you can be sitting pretty at seventy-five. If you can be sitting pretty in a state of unrelenting bereavement.

Gone. 'I'll just be gone for a while, Evie.' As if he might have simply said it. And so, any moment now . . .

She was to marry Ronnie that September, and hadn't her turn already arrived? Every night she decked herself out before a mirror bordered with glaring light bulbs that would be cruel now. At least her dressing-table mirror can be kindly angled and at least she can still summon up in it—it's not magic, it's merely memory—the tiara with the white plume, her carefully combed blonde fringe, the sparkling earrings, her bare powdered shoulders, the long white gloves almost reaching her armpits.

Beneath her then, extraordinarily, was the sea, swirling and splashing, and her silver sequins might have made her think of the glistening scales of fish, but she can't remember ever having had that thought then, even while the sea sploshed beneath her. Evie White: silvery and slippery as a fish.

The last thing she would put on was her smile, though did she really need to? Wasn't it just part of her, like her flashing blue eyes? In a moment she would get up and turn and, glancing over her shoulder, check herself from behind. She would place her palms on her hips, run her fingers under the rims of her tight costume, pull and pluck if necessary. She would give a little sober shimmy to test the other fanning plumes that might be called her tail. All this in a few seconds and by quick routine. Or she might use, in the same way, Ronnie as her mirror. Are my seams straight, Ronnie, are my feathers all right? Every night he might have this task and pleasure, but in a few moments the whole audience would have it. That was the idea.

The quivering feathers, no less than her smile or her eyes, would simply seem part of her.

Ronnie, meanwhile, would have given the final tweaks to his bow tie, pulled on his own white gloves. He would have put on his cape and checked its fastening. He would need to be able to undo and flourish his cape all in one movement. He would check everything he had in his pockets. That was important too. With his make-up on, his dark eyes would look all the more intense. He had become 'Pablo' now. She had become 'Eve'. With his make-up on too, his face would have acquired its peculiar stage gravity. She had to keep smiling and twirl and wiggle.

Neither of them had to speak. Or sing. Hadn't she found her perfect situation?

It was Jack who used to say that Ronnie in his stage get-up looked like Count Dracula's little brother. He never said what she looked like. Jack simply looked like Jack Robinson. But she used to imagine Ronnie privately (she never told him) as some swerving toreador, in a tight glittering costume to match her own. He had the red-lined cape after all and the bullfighter eyes. And the borrowed name. You would not believe this man came from Bethnal Green. And on stage he had the bold fluid movements too. He could dance in his own special way. She often thought that, whatever else their act was, it was a kind of dance, a ballet of silent intersecting actions. They never exactly planned it, it just happened.

Ronnie would change on stage. He had learnt to do it. A separate kind of magic.

'All set, Evie?'

He would place his hand under her feathers and give her silver backside a pat, a little squeeze. It was his privilege. Then they'd make their way up to the wings, to be in their positions behind the curtains, and before they got there they could already hear Jack doing his after-the-interval number, dancing and singing—he could do both things— in front of the curtains, in the silver spotlight, before it was their turn.

*By the light*

... tappity-tap tappity-tap ...

*Of the silvery moon*

... tappity-tap tappity-tap ...

*I like to spoon*

... tappity-tappity-tappity-tap ...



But life is unfair. Jack had died, exactly a year ago. In this bedroom, in the bed behind her. In the bed, beside her. She had not known he had died, since she was asleep. Perhaps he hadn't known either, for the same reason. She hoped so. It was the death we would all want.

But it was not, in her case, the awakening anyone would wish for. She hated remembering that awakening. Whenever it popped into her head, which it did constantly, she thrust it aside immediately. She often wished she might go to sleep and not wake up, just as Jack had done. But not wished.

George had rung last week and said, 'No pressure, Evie, no pressure at all, you may have other plans, you may want to be alone, but I haven't forgotten what day it is next Thursday. Would you like to have lunch? Would you like to raise a glass or two with me to the old boy?'

So she had put on her pearls and gone. She did not like George's expression 'old boy', but George, despite being—as Jack had sometimes affectionately called him—Jack's 'fast and loose' or 'wily' or even 'cut-throat' agent, was a kind, a considerate man.

And still the devoted agent of Jack's ghost.

Jack Robbins. Seventy-seven. Jack Robbins CBE. Never, quite, though there'd been talk, Sir Jack. Jack Robbins, the actor and even, in his heyday, occasional film star. Actor, then director, then producer, then actor-producer-director all in one and even with his own company. Rainbow

Productions. All it took, as he liked to say, unassumingly, was a couple of 'lucky hits' and everyone was laughing.

All the way to the bank. But he didn't say that, he left that implied. He always knew, in interviews, how to say just enough. Or to say nothing much really, but say it entertainingly. His company, but hers too. He liked to acknowledge it. 'Oh I have the most wonderful business partner, you see, and managing director. Wife actually.' The first two with a strong hint of a wink (the eyes now a little crinkly), the last with a rare unacted grateful directness.

'My wife is my inspiration, you see. I'd be nothing without her.'

Oh come off it, Jack, don't overdo it. But didn't it contain more than a grain of truth?

Jack Robbins. She could already feel him now—or the man the public knew—becoming a memory, a 'name'. Jack Robbins. Wasn't he in that TV show long ago? That sitcom that ran for ages. *Such is Life*. When he'd stopped doing variety, stopped calling himself Jack Robinson. When he'd changed into Terry Treadwell. Wasn't that his first big lucky break, the one that really got him an audience?

Break? Lucky? Don't you believe it. He was the one who said it was a lucky break. A favourite phrase. All modesty and innocence. But it was Evie White (sometimes known as Mrs Robbins) who'd put him there, Evie White who'd marched him down to Lime Grove and said, 'Sign, Jack, and say thank you to the nice people.'

She had flashed her smile. She had, too, a certain presence, a certain force. Jack had said, 'This is Evie White.' He hardly ever said 'Mrs Robbins'. And from that day on, until further notice, Jack became Terry Treadwell, and Jack Robinson faded even further into the past.

In the mirror she might see him now if she peered hard enough—he'd never really gone, just popped out—standing behind her, his hands on her shoulders, stooping to kiss them, each one, to kiss the nape of her neck, to clasp round her neck the pearls he'd given her. It was twenty years ago. These pearls that she'd just taken off, pearls for a pearl wedding.

Jack Robbins. Jack Robinson. Mr Nod-and-a-wink, Mr Make-'em-laugh, make-'em-smile, make-'em-swoon. Mr Moonlight. Just an old song-and-dance man, just an old handsome dreamboat, never short of a girl or three. But, as it turned out, an actor of surprising depth and range and, more surprising still, and all things being relative in the world of entertainment, a remarkably uxorious man.

She could vouch for it. Who would know better?

Listen to me, George, since we're here to honour the old boy: what's more extraordinary, that actors turn into these other people—how on earth is it done?—or that people anyway turn into people you never thought they might be?

Evie White. Chorus girl. Prancer and dancer. Up for anything really. Even one-time magician's assistant. But, as it turned out, hard-headed and sharp-eyed business woman. She could vouch for that too. And Jack Robbins' wife for nearly fifty years. Not Ronnie Deane's. Who would know better?

And what's more extraordinary: that magicians can turn things into other things, even make people disappear and appear again, or that people can anyway one day be there—oh so there—and the next day never be there again? Never.

She might have said such things over their lunch, but she didn't. And George might have listened and said, 'Well, that's quite a lot to chew on, Evie.'

All things being relative. And who cares about the famous two-week fling, back in the Seventies (Eddie Costello went to town on it in the *News of the World*), with a well-known rising actress (and where is she now, and what was her name again?). Did 'Mrs Robbins' (as Eddie called her) care? Jack came back, tail between his legs.

Did she care *now*? Come back, Jack, tail wherever you like.

And did she have any right, even then, to complain? How, after all, had their not-quite-fifty years begun? And who would have believed—was there no justice?—that they would have contained so much? Including even at least one kind of fiftieth, not so long after the launch of Rainbow Productions: Jack Robbins, fifty years on the stage. They had thrown a big party, in this house. She had ordered secretly a massive cake (never mind Jack's expanding waistline) and had specified that on it there should be, in gold icing, the two famous masks, but not in this case of comedy and tragedy—both masks must be smiling.

Jack, before cutting it, had demanded her assistance. So there had followed a flustered little performance, or competition, of hands. Whose hand should go on top to press down and guide the other's? Everyone had seen: it was like a wedding. And everyone had seen, despite the two smiling masks and the general laughter, the tears that had dripped for a second down Jack's face. Real tears, not actor's tears. No illusion.

Flash bulbs had popped. A riotous speech had followed. Oh the parties! The evenings! And one golden anniversary anyway.

Jack Robbins, who'd first trodden the boards in June 1945 in Cliftonville, Kent. She might picture it: tap shoes and a pint-sized penguin suit. Fourteen years old.

She fingers her pearls. His company and hers. More hers in fact. Now effectively all hers. She had always had the controlling share. His generous concession. 'Should anything happen to me, Evie . . .' Well it had. Rainbow Productions. It was their entirely private understanding that he had red, orange and yellow and she had blue, indigo and violet. And green. Why 'Rainbow Productions'? Never mind. It was well named. It had brought them a pot of gold. It had bought them Albany Square. And she had green, the middle and deciding colour, the controlling share.

Though hadn't she always had it? Long before Rainbow Productions was a twinkle in their eyes (but mainly hers). Hadn't she always wound Jack up and set him off in all the right directions? Just as his mother had done, just as her mother had done with her. The obituaries had simply noted the fact that they'd had no children. No 'survived bys'. Well, need she make any comment? Too busy with Jack, hands full with Jack. If it wasn't obvious.

Hadn't she made her move and placed her bet and hadn't it come good? Hadn't she once long ago when, yes, he was just a song-and-dance man and when they were all, really, just small glittery fish in a big sea, found the all-important little key in the small of his back and learnt how, carefully, lovingly, to turn it, when all the others were too busy just wrapping their legs around him?

Oh the things Ronnie would do to her, every night. For how many nights? A whole summer's worth. And for all to see. Or not exactly see. Not see at all. That was the whole point.

He would put her in a box and, while she was in it, take a sword—two, three swords—and run her through. But this was not before he'd put her in another box, all hunched up like a trussed turkey in an oven, and then locked the door, wielding first the magic key—the magic golden key!—and made her disappear. And then— another locking and relocking, another wielding of the key—made her come back again. That was kind of him. Only to run her through with swords.

But then he would put her in another box, lying down this time, her head sticking out at one end, her feet at the other. And he would take—no, he would brandish, he would wave it about—a saw. He would push one half of the box, the one with her head sticking out, round the stage, while the other half, with her legs, stayed put.

And if Evie White or 'Eve' didn't know how to sing, she knew how to scream, very convincingly (and this was her idea, challenging Ronnie's idea that the whole thing should be done in ghastly silence). Her scream could make them all gasp, sometimes even scream themselves. Her scream was worse than the saw.

Outside, on the pier, the punters could go on all sorts of contraptions—the dipper, the helter-skelter, the ghost train—that could make them scream too, scream with a kind of strange wild joy. Wasn't this, plainly, one of the reasons why people came on holiday—to be frightened to death? So didn't it all fit in with the general requirement: give them what they wanted?

When he locked her in that first box, all curled up, and her tail feathers got caught accidentally-on-purpose in the closing door she would give a little, a not so little, an audible 'Ooo!'. Which made them not know what to do: giggle or wince? And that was her idea too.

Oh the things she wouldn't submit to, the things she wouldn't go through for Ronnie (or, as he was at the time, Pablo). Yet the strangest thing of all was that amid all this savagery and torture she would maintain her indomitable and gleaming smile. She would, whenever the boxes were opened, step forth smiling, her tiara glinting, her arms flung up in their white gloves in a gesture of triumph and delight. She would cock one knee then the other and sway her hips, and whenever she had to move from one box to another, from one position of atrocity or mere jeopardy to another, she would do so with a similarly happy display of her shining invulnerable self.

The ring that shone on her finger, gold like the magic key, only made it inevitable that Ronnie would start making the joke, whenever he introduced her to anyone who'd seen the show, 'Meet Evie. Meet Eve. My other half. Halves.'

And if Jack, as planned, had been best man at their wedding that September he'd surely have stolen Ronnie's joke, perhaps not preventing himself for a moment from slipping back into the role of Jack Robinson. 'Please join me, folks, boys and girls, in drinking to Ronnie's other half. Or should I say halves? May he always keep putting her back together again.'

Instead he stole a great deal more.

Brighton Town Hall, the Registry Office. It still might have happened, that September, if everything else had been put back together again.

And she would have been—another line for Jack?—
'married to magic'. As she would by then have understood
that Ronnie was too, long before he was married to her.

But what was wrong with that? Wasn't it what had
lured her in the first place? Magician's Assistant Wanted.

And did she find out anyway the answer to that central
and enticing question? Magic: so how was it done then?

If anyone ought to have found out, it was her. But here
was the crucial catch. If she'd found out, if she'd known,
she could never have told, could she? Because that was
the deal, the pledge, more binding and unbreakable, it
seemed, than even a promise of marriage. So how would
anyone ever *know* whether she knew or didn't?

She looks into her mirror now as if the only person she
might tell is the one staring back at her. But even that
would be telling, wouldn't it? She'd never even told Jack,
though he'd pressed her a few times, before letting the
whole thing go and pass into history. It's what everyone
wants to know. How is it done? 'Come on, Evie, you can
tell me. Surely you can tell me *now*. I won't tell anyone else.'

He was like a man wanting to know about other men

she'd slept with. Specifically in this case Ronnie Deane (all the others had passed into their own histories). But she wasn't telling—either way. Did she ask what it had been like with Flora? All the Floras. Tell me about all that magic that went on with Flora. A new trick with each one?

She knew how most of the tricks were done with Ronnie, of course she did, but that wasn't the point. And for some reason still wasn't, even now.

Would Ronnie have ever told the world?

In those days, in 1959, there were plenty of beaches, though Brighton wasn't one of them, with bits of rusted ironwork and lumps of concrete sticking up out of them and signs saying 'Danger! Mines – Keep Out'. And there were plenty of people walking about who would never open their mouths about certain things. They'd signed up, taken the oath. And as with Official Secrets, so with magic. A condition for life.

Sorry. Can't talk. Lips sealed. No, you won't get it out of me, not even if you stick swords through me, not even if you saw me in half.

'Oh come on, Evie!' What had she been *doing* inside all those boxes? Leaving it to Ronnie?

But yes, more often than not, that's exactly how it

was, and even when she'd learnt how things were done it didn't exactly stop her wondering, having her doubts. In some ways the more she knew the more she wondered. Then it would be Ronnie who would have to say, 'It's all right, Evie, you can trust me. Just do as I say. Just get in and leave it to me. You don't have to worry at all. I'm never going to hurt you.'

Nor did he. It was never that way round.

And only once, during their early rehearsing at the Belmont (one day there was a whole array of collapsible yet forbidding boxes in which it seemed she was going to be successively confined), did she ever say, from inside, in the darkness, 'Ronnie—are you still there?' She couldn't help it. It was an involuntary cry—it had nothing to do with magic—squeezed from her suddenly palpitating heart. And Ronnie had said, and it was just as well he said it, in a rather far-off voice, 'Yes I am, Evie. I'm here.' It had seemed to her, from where she was, that Ronnie too might have been speaking from inside some dark box and that he was uttering something just as irrepressibly issuing from deep inside himself.

It had seemed—and this must have been long before he slipped an engagement ring on her finger, though not long after she'd said that thing about his eyes—that some bond had just been formed between them of a kind not usually made, or even possible, between two people.

She can't remember Ronnie ever saying, 'Evie—are you still there?' Of course he didn't need to. It was a sign of his power and his trust. But perhaps he should have asked it nonetheless.

And how do you ever explain to anyone what it's like to be levitating? Ronnie had said to her one day, 'Now you are levitating, Evie. Trust me, you are levitating.' She could only say what it felt like at the time: that yes she was and no she couldn't possibly be. And what a strange thing to be doing, to be having happen to you, a kind of gift or privilege, what a strange word even. Had she ever known—though she hadn't known so many things—that in her life she would one day levitate? *Levitate*!

But there they were anyway that summer, night after night, waiting behind the curtains to go on, waiting to be 'Pablo and Eve', sometimes drawing deep insistent breaths that the audience would never see and sometimes—the audience would never see it either and it was something else she would never tell—holding out to each other a clutching reassuring hand.

While in front of the curtains Jack would be finishing his number.

*Oh honeymoon, keep a-shinin' in June!*

Sometimes, outside, after the show, there might be that real and actual magic—a silvery moon hanging over the water, glimmering on the waves as they broke on the shingle. If the rain wasn't bucketing down or a gale blowing.

She would walk back along the boards, arm in arm with Ronnie, no longer Pablo and Eve, just Ronnie and Evie, just another holidaying couple it might seem. Though sometimes they were recognised, and it was often her they spotted first. 'Aren't you—?' 'Yes, Eve. Yes. And this is Pablo.' She would never say 'Ronnie' and she couldn't make the joke, the equivalent one, that Ronnie could make of her.

These moments when they were recognised made her proud. Ronnie might seem a little annoyed, a little aloof, and she'd tell him that was a bad attitude (she had already become a bit of a manager). He should always smile, smile, be nice to the people. They might look at him and she could hear them thinking: That's Pablo? Really? And then thinking: But, yes, on second thoughts, that's him.

It was surely a good sign if they could be spotted, even just on the pier. Their act must be doing well, they were 'known'. And Ronnie began to develop anyway, over the weeks, a certain off-stage aura and style, a way of being at ease in himself, and she liked to think that some of this was because of her.

Sometimes she'd think, who needed magic, or even a stage or a costume, if she had this? Didn't she have all a girl might want? And she'd think, even with a sort of pity, of the latest doomed girl hanging on Jack's arm.

Jack would say, leaning on the rail with them, with or without some girl, and looking at the glinting waves, 'You won't get any of this, I'll tell you, at the Palladium or the Hackney fucking Empire. You'll get a nice little stroll down piss alley.'

Once he said, in the dressing room, when for some reason everything went quiet and they could hear the soft churning sound in their ears, 'No, that's not the waves, playmates, that's the sound of tonight's audience gnashing their teeth already.'

He was only twenty-eight, same age as Ronnie, and none of them knew then what was coming, but it was part of his function to act older than his age. He was master of ceremonies, and daddy to them all. Take it from him, he'd been around, he'd seen everything.

And it was strange how in all those shows, all those

performances, a whole season's worth, you hardly stopped to think—she never thought about it as she looked at her face in the mirror and placed the tiara, like a regular coronation, in her hair: The sea is right beneath us now. Right beneath us now the waves are swishing and swirling, the fish are darting, the seaweed is swaying this way and that. If the stage were to open up we'd all go tumbling through into the water.

Jack Robbins was 'Jack Robinson' then. In his time he would play too many roles to count or remember. Some would slip over him and be gone like mere tryings-on—the cameo parts in films—but some would stick and the problem would be how to get rid of them. How to convince the punters who recognised him on the street (it would happen) that he and they were not the same person.

Or rather, sometimes, how not. How to inwardly grit the teeth while outwardly grinning, and take that little invisible step—they wouldn't see it—and give them the catchphrases, the lines, the gestures and faces that they wanted. Amazing! Like that chancer-cum-clown-cum-hard-pressed-family-man, Terry Treadwell in *Such is Life*, the show that put him, according to George Cohen, 'before the nation'. And Evie didn't disagree.

If Evie was there—with the punters and pesterers, the autograph-seekers—he might feel her little prod, her squeeze of his elbow, but even if she wasn't he would hear her whisper in his ear. 'Go on, Jack. Do it. One more time. Be Terry Treadwell.'

The show that put quite a lot of dosh in the bank, and quite a lot of it in George's. And made his name. Jack Robbins. Or Terry Treadwell. Which bloody one was he?

But one day, finally, he somehow got out of 'being' Terry Treadwell, or Terry Treadwell, poor man, just ceased to 'be' himself. He wouldn't like to put a date on when Terry Treadwell expired. He'd had his time, poor fool, then just slipped into memory. Wasn't Jack Robbins in that sitcom thing, years ago? What was the name of it, what was that character again? Tommy somebody, Teddy somebody?

Other roles would come and some of them he would just enter like a dream, he would just float in them as if they'd always been waiting for him. Like his first big Shakespearean role, Puck in *A Midsummer Night's Dream*.

Speaking of dreams. Puck. No jokes please. He was a 'brilliant Puck'. A revelation. Was this the same man, they asked, who'd been Terry Treadwell? Well yes, it was.

But that too would pass into memory. Wasn't he Puck once, at Stratford, a great Puck (or, as he'd liked pedantically to point out, Robin Goodfellow).

And no smutty jokes please. My wife always thought I could be a great Puck, if I really tried. Like, before her, too many girls to remember. But none after. Seriously.

So who was ever going to remember Jack Robinson? Especially as that summer, that September, Jack Robinson simply ceased to be too, simply sidled away, his time was up, never to return. Who was going to remember? Except himself of course, publicly but cryptically, every time he said, 'Oh just an old song-and-dance man.'

'I was brought up on variety, you know. Spice of life. All a long time ago. Acting? You must be joking.'

But there he'd been, standing in the wings, and there was no other role for him. And this wasn't just some part written by someone else like those he'd be offered in the future, of which George might say—but there was no

George then—'This might interest you, sunshine.' He had invented Jack Robinson himself. How the hell had that happened? His own stupid fault. And now he had to *be* him. Every bloody show. It wasn't acting? And by now, of course, they all believed he *was* him. And he loved and he hated the poor strutting bastard.

Now some of them were even starting to shout, 'Where's Jack?! Where's Jack?!' Well it was his own name, so which one did they mean? 'Where's Jack?!' What a fucking rabble.

Some people, stage hands, seeing him standing there frozen in the wings, would think he was just milking it. There he goes again. They couldn't see that it was one of those nights when it wasn't just a step, it was a cliff edge, and he was sick with confusion and terror. And there was no one to push him. Except himself of course. Or once upon a time his mother, who'd hopped it long ago with a garage owner. A garage owner! I ask you, folks. His mother who'd once done music hall, who'd once been known among other names (shy little dairymaid as she'd been) as Betty Butter. *'I'm Betty Butter and I'm all of a-flutter . . .'* So she had sung once.

And there was no Evie to give him the shove. Not yet, not yet. How did you push yourself in the back?

'Where's Jack?! Where's Jack?!' They would turn it into a chant soon, and of course everyone thought it was wonderful—even he thought it was wonderful—he was milking it, creaming it, lapping it up. 'Where's Jack?!'

And then it would happen. How did it happen? He stepped off the edge, but was still there. Not plummeting. There was the bath of the stage lights and then, just for doing it, just for walking on, it seemed, the sea of applause. And then, before you could say—

'Here I am! Here I am! Well I never! Well I thought I could hear someone calling. Well, are you all having a *good time*?'

'*Ye-es*!!'

'Well in that case I'll be off then!'

He was Jack Robinson. Who else? And what would the show have been without him? Some people would have said he *was* the show. And yet as compere he was, like no one else, constantly in and out of it. He stepped forward from it, in front of the curtains, to have his little chats with them, to be their old mate, their old pal, then slipped back into it to do one of his numbers. Or to disappear for whole stretches—where's Jack?—and then be back again. And he never failed to be there at the end to give them his goodnight gab and sing them his song.

'So it's goodnight, boys and girls, and it's *buenas noches* for anyone from foreign parts, and mind how you go, folks, out there on the boards in the dark. It's hard enough, I tell you, treading the boards up here . . .'

But sometimes when he disappeared he didn't just loiter backstage or go to the dressing room to pat off the sweat, or go outside to stand on the little screened-off bit reserved for the theatre company, to lean on the rails and flick cigarette ash into the waves and be himself (himself?) for a while.

Instead he'd cross another kind of line. He'd weave his way from backstage to front-of-house, or not quite. There was a route you could take. He'd emerge again in the darkness at the back of the stalls, while the show was still going on—and, look, it could carry on quite happily without him. He'd blend in quietly with the audience and if anyone saw he'd make a showy furtive thing of it. A finger to his lips. Yes, it's me, but you never saw me, okay?

He'd sit in one of the empty seats in the back row, though there were fewer of these now, he noted, now the season had progressed. It was nearly August. And if there were no seats at all he'd just lean on the back wall or take one of the jump-seats used by the usherettes. He'd do the finger-to-the-lips thing for the usherette.

And one of those usherettes, by the way—but that was another story.

And he'd watch. If anyone observed carefully these visits of his—but they'd have to be one of those weird regulars, those gluttons for punishment as he was known to call them—they'd notice it was always the same act he chose to watch. Pablo and Eve. First spot after the interval. He'd just been up there in fact, to introduce them—'And now, boys and girls'—and now he was down here, just one of them.

'And now here's something you're not going to believe . . .'

And he'd better make sure he was up there again in a little while for when their act was finished.

'Didn't I tell you, folks, didn't I say . . .?'

He'd sit and he'd watch and he'd wonder perhaps along with all the others how the tricks were done. But it wasn't Ronnie—or Pablo—he was really watching. Of course not. Down here at the back of the auditorium he was part of the audience and he wasn't. He was Jack Robinson and he wasn't. He wasn't even Jack Robbins.

In the darkness, neither in nor out of the audience,

he would sometimes feel the thinness, the fakery of the plush rapt edifice around him. Plush? Turn up the lights and you'd soon see, he knew, how tatty, how shabby, how sham it all was. How it all depended on some stretch of the mind. Sometimes, beyond the stirrings and gaspings of the audience, he might think he could hear the creakings and strainings of the pier itself, like a big foundering ship. But perhaps it was more that he was the one who was going under.

Why did he make these furtive forays? Just to see what it was like, to get the effect, without all the behind-the-scenes contrivance? To be a spy and report back? Of course not. He simply needed to watch her, unobserved. Forget 'Pablo and Eve'. Forget Pablo, forget Ronnie. Forget even all this stuff they were doing together. It was simply her. He'd stepped over a different edge and he could feel himself slipping, losing himself. All the girls, but he wanted her. He could feel himself going down like a drowning man.

Evie looks in the mirror. Her lips are sealed. Her lips are anyway a diminished version of what they'd once been.

And if no one could say—or wouldn't say—then how did anyone know there was such a thing in the first place: magic? All done by mirrors.

But that would leave a big question, wouldn't it? If there was no such thing as magic, why become a magician?

One night after a long day in the rehearsal room behind the Belmont Theatre they'd gone back to his place and snuggled up together. It had been bound to happen sooner or later. Had it happened by magic—because Ronnie, being what he was, had made it happen? Not if she was Evie White it hadn't, not if she'd had anything to do with it. But then would it be right to say—it would certainly be a shame—that there was nothing magical about it? Would it be wrong to say that they'd put each other under a bit of a spell?

And—to jump ahead—did Ronnie produce that ring because he just wanted to be sure, he wanted to keep what he'd caught? If he was a magician, why should he have needed to do that? Or did he produce it because she'd done something that must have seemed magical, even to him? It had made those eyes of his go suddenly wide as plates. He'd asked her a question, a question he'd never asked before in his life, and she'd said, really quite quickly, 'Yes, Ronnie, yes!' She'd said that word before, too many times to count, but she'd never said it like that—the biggest yes so far of her twenty-five-year life.

So: hey presto!

But one thing at a time. They'd gone back to his place. His place was a grubby little flat, but not as grubby or as little as she'd expected (that windfall again?), and anyway she'd seen worse. It was November and it was cold, one of those raw winter afternoons when night seems to fall at three o'clock. While they'd held each other, an electric fire, a Belling portable positioned not far away on the floor with its bars blazing, had thrown its warmth and its glow upon them. Now and then it clicked and twanged.

But what do you do afterwards? At least for a while you talk. Her palm had circled over his chest. It was not a bad little chest, and not so little either, and now she had the privilege of touching it and viewing it closely, she could see it came with just the right amount of not too long or thick or curly hairs. Under her hand they had a pleasing roughness-yet-silkiness, and in the light from the fire they shone with, here and there, a coppery spark.

'So why magic, Ronnie? How did it all begin?'

He did not say, as she herself might have said in answer to most questions about her life, 'My mother.' But they would get round to his mother eventually. He was not a shy or hesitant man (what were they doing right then?), but he could be very careful about some things. You had to draw them gently out of him.

It seemed that Ronnie had become a magician more by chance than intention, though once the seed was sown, the wish had taken hold of him completely. Perhaps the sowing of the seed was itself a stroke of magic.

'Where was this, Ronnie?'

She caressed his chest. She was, herself, about to become not a little enchanted.

'It was at a place called Evergrene.'

'Evergrene?'

'Evergrene.'

He said it with a big full stop. He said it as if he might also have said, 'And doesn't everyone know about Evergrene? And doesn't that explain everything?'

'You'll have to do a bit better than that. You'll have to tell me where Evergrene is.'

'It's in Oxfordshire. It was where I was in the war. You're talking to a fully qualified evacuee. How about you?'

She quickly dealt with that. No, never an evacuee. She and her mum had stuck it out in Woking. A long way from the docks, and—look—no damage. Besides, her mother had had her daughter's theatrical career to think about. 'This war will be over one day, Evie, and then what? Then what?' But this was her story, it could wait.

No, she'd never been an evacuee. Though now she was rather beginning to wish she had.

'Come on, Ronnie. Evergrene.'

It seemed from the way he began so cagily to speak about it that it might have been a six-year holiday, that it might have been where—all before there were hairs on his chest—he'd had the time of his life. He was reluctant to talk about it perhaps because it all sounded too good to be true. It did. Perhaps he was making it all up and having her on. But it gradually dawned on her that he spoke about these years of his life with such shiftiness and struggle because he'd never spoken about them to anyone before. She was the one, she was the first.

And must also have been the last.

She would never anyway have any other source or corroboration for her knowledge of the life of Ronnie Deane than Jack Robbins. Hadn't Jack known him for something like ten years? But she would be able to tell at once that it was more the other way round. Jack might know a hundred things that she didn't, but he didn't know these things that Ronnie had told only her and that she, in turn, would never tell Jack.

Jack would only say, making a little bundle of jokes of it, 'He went to Oxford, Evie. Cut above. He took a degree in magic. He met the Wizard of Oxford. Sorcerer's apprentice.'

In any case she was yet to meet Jack Robbins.

She stroked Ronnie's chest, feeling that—despite the hairs—she might be stroking the chest of an eight-, a nine-year-old boy.

It turned out that he'd had two childhoods—almost, you might say, two lives—and the second had taken over from the first. He'd been taken in by this couple called the Lawrences and raised by them as if he were their own. And, to cap it all, Mr Lawrence, Eric Lawrence, had turned out to be a temporarily underoccupied magician.

But then the war had come to an end and this—what to call it?—magical life had had to stop, even go into reverse. Or not exactly, since Ronnie wanted to be a magician too and, up to a point, already was one.

It was not so difficult now to guess, before Ronnie told her, that Ronnie's 'little windfall', of which she herself was an indirect beneficiary, had come from this same Eric Lawrence, who, he said, had recently died. It became gradually apparent that another reason why all this information was emerging with such painfulness from Ronnie was that he was still in a state of mourning.

She wouldn't be lying here—they wouldn't be lying here—without Eric Lawrence's money. Never mind magic.

But it wasn't as simple as that. She wanted to ask about the rest of Ronnie's childhood, the 'real' one. There was so much, it seemed, he was still keeping from her.

And how anyway—to jump forward—had he got to call himself Pablo?

'It's my middle name, isn't it, it's my real name? My middle name is Paul.'

'Yes. But.'

He said, 'Spanish blood, Evie.'

Which was almost as mysterious as his saying 'Evergrene'.

Though, yes, to look at him—and she was having a good look at him now—you might have guessed that too. Those eyes in particular.

'Don't laugh, Evie, but my mother's middle name is Dolores.'

Well that was something, and it conjured up in her mind an image of Ronnie's mother—colourful, exotic, even theatrical—that made her quite want to meet her, and even made her think that her own mother, who was only called Mabel, might like to meet her too.

But this was seriously to jump ahead, and how wrong she was.

'So where is she now, Ronnie, your mother? What does she do?'

'She's a couple of miles from where we are now. She's a charwoman in Bethnal Green. Do you want to go and see her?'

It was the only time, as it would turn out, that Ronnie would extend this invitation, and it was clear that he didn't really mean it. It was also of course the last thing she wanted to do at that moment.

'No, not just now, Ronnie.'

But later, when she had time to think about it, it was not difficult to put herself in Mrs Deane's shoes and imagine how it would have felt to receive back her one and only son in Bethnal Green and discover that he'd changed altogether. Not just changed, he wanted to be a magician.

It didn't take much to see that there had been a rift.

And a rift that had only widened when Ronnie attempted to repair it. This all suddenly escaped from him too that afternoon, while the electric fire continued its pinging and buzzing.

When the all-important windfall had come his way—and they were now up to very recent times—he had, with the best of motives, offered the larger part of it to his mother, by way of recompense for all damage and division. But his mother had refused it. She had even, as it were, thrown it back in his face. Strong words had been spoken.

Ronnie had used another expression which it seemed he'd been storing up. 'Spanish passion, Evie.'

And did she still want to pop round and see her?

'What's her first name, Ronnie?'

'Agnes.'

Agnes Dolores. It made the mind again paint pictures.

'And your father?'

There was a long pause. It was a simple question.

'Sid.'

There was another long pause.

'He's at the bottom of the sea, Evie. Merchant navy. 1940.'

And that closed the conversation. But at least they were more or less as one there. She couldn't give as many facts about her own father. For all she knew of his whereabouts (she believed he had been called Bill), he might as well have been at the bottom of the sea too.

Poor Agnes. Poor Mabel.

She never disclosed any of this to her own mother. One thing at a time. And time enough, she would think, for Ronnie perhaps to get round to telling her himself. First she had to tell her mother about Ronnie anyway, and she left that for a while, to be sure of her ground. But one day, using one of the phones at the Belmont Theatre, she said, 'Guess what, Mum, I'm working with a magician.'

And then, not so very long after that, she said, 'Guess what, Mum, I'm going to marry him.'

This was not perhaps what every mother wants to hear from her only daughter, but her mother's answer was simple and heartfelt. 'Oh how wonderful, sweetheart. And when am I going to meet him?'

No such breathless messages ever passed, it seemed,

between Ronnie and his mother. She would come to wonder if Ronnie's mother ever knew of her future daughter-in-law's existence. And just as well, she would also come to think.

Yet for a few fond months of her life she, Evie White, was the fool who thought that her impending marriage to Ronnie might achieve two ends. She would, of course, marry Ronnie. But might not this happy union, even in prospect, be the means of bringing about a happy reunion between mother and son? When she pictured Ronnie's mother, she pictured two mothers at bitter war with each other in the same person. One called Agnes, with a heart of stone, one called Dolores, with a heart only waiting to melt.

She, Evie White, with a heart, she thought, that was simple and undivided, was a fool for ever making (of someone she'd never met) such a childish analysis. A fool for ever believing in such hokum.

One morning in early July 1959, two weeks into the season, Mabel White stepped off the Brighton Belle onto Brighton Station. She carried a small white suitcase, wore a loudly cheerful summer frock (both things newly purchased) and a sunhat that seemed to come with its own small garden. She strode boldly down the platform, pausing halfway to give a look of sudden joy followed by some vigorous waving.

Here was a woman who knew how to make an entrance and who clearly intended to enjoy herself during her seaside weekend. The nervousness Evie had felt as she waited with Ronnie at the barrier fled before this vivid approaching presence. As Evie well knew, Mabel had had her disappointments, yet here she was, almost fifty, like a brash sea breeze herself.

She might have turned to Ronnie and said, as if fulfilling her part of a bargain, 'There you are, that's *my* mother for you.'

But soon she was saying, while Mabel beamed, 'Mum, this is Ronnie.'

Evie didn't know (and never would) the particular associations that railway stations and mothers held for Ronnie, that his own nervousness was complicated, but she could see from the sometimes daunted look on his face during this otherwise bracing visit that Ronnie's mother and her own must be a million miles apart.

And had Mabel really taken to Ronnie?

'So this is—the magician!'

Her mother was always direct. She wore a pair of little white gloves.

After the show that evening—'Oh but you were amazing, darlings!'—when Mabel was introduced to Jack, it became clear to Evie that, had her mother been twenty years younger, she might have readily joined the line of Floras. She whispered in Evie's ear, 'He's a one, isn't he?' Meaning Jack, not Ronnie.

It was late and her mother was a little drunk—this was in the bar of the seafront hotel they'd booked for her—and might have been forgiven for forgetting the chief purpose of her visit to Brighton, but Evie had felt momentarily troubled. She told herself that her mum and Jack were getting along like a house on fire because Jack, as she knew by now, also had a 'theatrical' mother. But this only raised again the issue of how different Ronnie's mother must be. She wondered how Ronnie must feel, sitting there while his mother-in-law-to-be made eyes at Jack, and she reached under the table to squeeze Ronnie's hand.

When they'd seen Mabel off at the station she had showered them both with kisses and called them her 'chickens'. The weekend had been a general success, but it had underscored a problem. To Evie, invigorated by her mother's undiminished buoyancy, the solution seemed obvious. Surely an equivalent visit by Ronnie's mother was needed. Evie was prepared to take on all the challenges and even saw herself as being—with the help of sea air and free tickets to the show—the agent of reconciliation. She had her own share of her mother's sunniness.

But she soon stopped putting forward her suggestion. It was plain, for all the enthusiasm Ronnie expressed for it, that such a visit was never going to happen. She stopped asking about Ronnie's mother, though she did not stop thinking about her, forming stern pictures of her and comparing them with those so recently reprinted of her own mother, and wondering—fingering her engagement ring—what she might be getting into.

It was her first teetering. Why had she said her yes so quickly?

She heard her mother's words again—no one else had heard them—tickling in her ear: 'He's a one, isn't he?'

Surely she would have to meet Ronnie's mum somehow—somewhere—some time? But this line of thinking was soon replaced by a whole different kind of questioning. To this day, sitting alone in her bedroom, she can never have the answer, though the question stays with her.

How could she know—how could either of them know—that Mrs Deane *hadn't* in fact come to Brighton? Hadn't come, secretly and of her own accord, to see for herself this woman her son had chosen, and at the same time to see all this nonsense, this magic poppycock that he got up to. There was a simple way of achieving all this. All she had to do was get the train to Brighton, buy a ticket for the show and slip in unnoticed.

Had she sat, hidden in the dark, and cast her stony judgement on the two of them, on the whole ridiculous enterprise, and then slipped out again? They would never have known that her eyes were upon them.

And what might she have thought while she sat there? That's my Ronnie up there, calling himself 'Pablo' and sawing his future wife in half. A fine way of going about getting married. And who's she, anyway, when she's at home, the one with all the sequins and feathers and precious little else, looking like she'll never stop smiling?

But then it became clear, though there was still about half of the season left and their act was going from strength to strength, that, whether she'd done this or not, she wouldn't be coming now anyway, secretly or otherwise, because Mrs Deane—Agnes Dolores Deane—had died.

The show must always go on, but sometimes things happen and it can't. It was now early August, the crowds were thickening in Brighton and the audiences for the pier show were swelling. When Jack slipped back to do his watching there might be no spare seats. And by now there was no denying it, 'Pablo and Eve' had become one of the top attractions. On the billboards their names now appeared higher up and in larger lettering, and crude little photographed faces—Pablo fiercely staring, Eve serenely smiling—floated beside them.

Eddie Costello, in his Arts and Entertainments column, had waggishly put it that 'They not only did magic but they had it.' And had added that one should hope so too, since it was no secret they were engaged to be married. This little fairy tale hovered round their act like some parallel piece of conjuring. And no harm in it surely, since it was true. Though it was not true, as Eddie had implied, that theirs was a Brighton romance, that they'd met on the pier, as it were, and plighted their troth to the sound of the waves. But let Brighton believe it. Only Ronnie and Evie—or Pablo and Eve—might know that they'd plighted their troth, to all intents and purposes, in Finsbury, off the City Road, in the glow of a Belling portable.

And, anyway, the tricks (as everyone called them, you can't stop people calling them tricks) were quite something, and were performed now with an ever slicker and more adventurous style. Ronnie, to the disappointment of some, had begun scaling down all that stuff with boxes and swords—'old-hat stuff' he called it—and was bringing into the act more things with his own—their own—trademark upon them. Things you couldn't get from other magicians. He was taking risks perhaps, but it was working. Give the people what they want, yes, but why not give them something truly amazing?

In short, though only Ronnie himself could have put it this way, he was moving from magic towards wizardry. There was a difference, a difference in ambition, but a difference in the very nature of the two things. There was a perilous line between the two, and Ronnie recognised in himself the ability to cross it. He could see the land of wizardry beckoning to him. Who knew what lay in it? And perhaps there might be no stepping back. And it was not simply a show-business region, he knew this, it was a different world altogether, it had different laws, it made different demands. But he was still young, and who knew what he might yet be capable of?

As he contemplated his progress to this other zone only one thing, and it was not a lack of courage, made him pause. How might he take Evie with him? How might he—and should he even—reach out his hand to her and ask her to take this leap with him? Yet how could he not? He did not underestimate his own powers and yet he knew now, it had become a fact of life, that he could not do anything without her.

Beneath his growing on-stage bravura, he was torn and confounded. Eric Lawrence, though he had imparted many words of wisdom, had never said, 'Get yourself an assistant.' That had been Jack's idea. So how, Ronnie had sometimes wondered but never felt able to ask, had Eric found his Penny?

While Evie never ceased to sparkle on stage, he could sometimes see a troubled look in her eyes, like someone hesitating to jump. Their rehearsals, when he tried to teach her his latest wild idea, became edgy. 'It's beyond me,' Evie would say or, 'You're losing me, Ronnie.'

He remembered how she'd said, with such excitement in her face, that it was all 'a new departure' for her too.

Sometimes during the show Ronnie's eyes would take on a quite possessed quality. He might fix the audience with them, as if to say, 'You think I can't do this, you think this can't happen?' Yet to his smouldering concentration Evie's smiling radiance provided exactly the right balance. To the audience it seemed—and what else mattered?—that they simply worked together, and amazed together. It would be hard to say exactly when each new 'trick' (to use that word) was added and an old one dropped away. The act had become a fluid phenomenon, yet full of a thrilling tension. You never knew what might happen next. This in itself became part of the attraction.

The billboards now carried above their names the little embellishment, 'Come and See!' But one day—it was simply a sudden idea of Jack's—there was something much bolder.

'Why don't you call yourself the *Great* Pablo, Ronnie? Why don't you think big?'

Ronnie had looked for a while at his friend, but in the circumstances hadn't objected. Nor had the show's presenters. Nor had Brighton and its holiday-making public.

'Come and See! Come and See the Great Pablo!'

But Eve was always just Eve. And Jack was just Jack.

'And now, folks, I want you to see something that

will make your eyes pop, something you're not going to believe. I want you to meet a very special friend of mine, the Great—yes I said the Great—Pablo! He doesn't talk very much, but you'll see why he doesn't need to. And I want you to meet—and she'll make your eyes pop too, gents—the delightful, the delectable, the delorious—Eve!'

It would be hard to say exactly when Ronnie began to think about one big trick, one sensational feat to really make them the talk of the town. But it must have been around the time that he metamorphosed into the Great Pablo. Was it before or after those two shows that, to the dismay of the theatre-goers, he and Evie were regrettably compelled to miss? When exactly was that? It would anyway seem—it was almost like some canny piece of stagecraft itself—that Pablo had only made himself scarce for forty-eight hours in order to return with new force and in new form as the Great Pablo. And, yes, with another new trick. And quite a trick too.

He had never liked the word, even despised it. It was perhaps around this time—when he was assuming greatness—that he made his views on the matter particularly plain, one day in the Walpole. Or he put a new slant on them. He said *people* did tricks, didn't they, all the time?

People were always playing tricks. But magicians—he'd say it one more time—did illusions. And when, after saying this, he'd gone to the bar in something of a huff to fetch drinks, Jack had leant over to Evie and said, 'Tricks? Illusions? What's the difference, Evie? You tell me.' He'd leant close enough to make it a whisper and as his breath brushed her ear he'd thought for a moment of the sound of the sea they say you can hear in a shell. And then he'd thought that you couldn't call that a trick, the right word was illusion, but he didn't take back what he'd just said to Evie.

It was unfortunate anyway that it was around this time that Ronnie got word from a hospital in London that his mother was ill. The actual words were 'gravely ill'. It was one of those messages in a readily understood code: 'You'd better come at once, or you might never—'

It was a heart condition. He thought of Eric Lawrence's 'dicky ticker', as if there might have been some bizarre connection. Ronnie had never known that his mother had a heart condition. Nor, presumably, had she. And he had almost forgotten that he'd sent her a phone number where she could contact him, if for any reason . . .

These unspecified reasons might have included a sudden wish (never before expressed) to come and see her son performing in a show, and at the same time meet the woman who was going to be his wife—things which might have swelled both a mother's and a son's heart. But whether Ronnie had ever actually extended such an invitation to his mother or whether he had even told her that he was now engaged to be married, only Ronnie knew.

There had been no telephone calls, either way, until now, but he supposed that his mother must have given the number to the hospital people or that they'd simply discovered it somehow. He was that person he'd never before thought of himself as being: 'next of kin'.

Had his mother, in her dire situation, wanted him to know? 'My Ronnie must be told.' He would never know this. Even as he answered this sobering phone call he thought of all those calls that had never been made between them when they were apart in the war. But they had been apart ever since really. Then he thought—it seemed like yesterday—of those white handkerchiefs being waved by all the mothers while he was being bundled onto his train. A sudden snow of handkerchiefs:

he couldn't tell which one, if any, was hers. Then he thought of her hand squeezing his when she'd left him at the school gates.

'Tell her I'm on my way.'

What else could he say? 'I am a magician'? Tell her that I'm coming with my magic wand. And even my supply of special white handkerchiefs.

Yet at once he'd thought of that evening's performance. He couldn't just cancel it, surely? But Evie said and Jack said too that there was no alternative, he had to go and be with his mother. They were suddenly like this other couple telling him what to do. Which only raised another question. Was Evie going to come with him? Was Evie, his future wife, who'd never met his mother, going to come with him when he went to see his mother, perhaps for the last time?

He did not ask. She did not say. It was not a test, but it seemed that she would not be accompanying him, and, all things considered, he could see her point of view. He was not going to demand it. But he suddenly felt very alone and Evie seemed to recede from him and become hard to discern, as if she were now the one seeing him off while he had to board some ominous train. Which was almost literally the case.

They said he must go. Jack said he shouldn't give it a second thought. He would make a special announcement, of course. He would use that word that gets used in the theatre to cover all kinds of eventualities: 'indisposed'. It was one of those words, like the phrase 'next of kin', that do not crop up often, yet sometimes have their moment.

Then Jack said, 'Unless you think Evie and I should do the act for you.' It was a bad joke in circumstances when no jokes were needed, a bad attempt to lighten a fraught situation. But he had said it.

So Ronnie Deane found himself on a train to London, and, though it was all the other way round and he had been an adult for years, he couldn't help feeling he was really eight years old and that in some way, perhaps, he always had been. He had never grown up. He was an evacuee, there was a sort of war on again, he was on a train, but this time he was travelling towards his mother. And it was just as bad.

The difference was that when he was eight years old he had not known about magic, it had not yet come into his view. And he thought again, as he travelled towards his mother, of the absurdity and uselessness of this thing that he had nonetheless chosen to make the object of his life.

'Magic, Ronnie, whatever fucking next?'

What next indeed? It was early August. Sussex—ripe, green, drowsy with summer—floated by, and he was travelling in the wrong direction, away from the coast, away from that happy ribbon of land set aside for holidays and fun, where people wanted, at least just once every year, only to be entertained, to play.

It had been his awkward situation now and then—sometimes on trains—to find himself in a brief conversation with a stranger in which the innocuous question arose: 'So what do you do then?' Sometimes he had lied. But mostly, intrepidly, he had told the truth. The word wasn't difficult in itself.

Then they of course might think he was lying. 'You're having me on.' Or they'd want him immediately to 'do a trick'. To prove it. Or the conversation might drift into some wishful realm in which it was assumed he might do *anything*. Sort out this man's problems, for example. Make money grow on trees, make dreams come true. Come on then, if you're what you say you are. And there would be an evident disappointment, even a touch of suspicion and distrust if it emerged, as it would, that he could not do absolutely anything, there were only some things he could do.

Call yourself a magician . . .

It was depressing, even belittling. How easy, even enviable to be able to say you were a plumber or a travelling salesman. How easy it had been when he was in the army, in a uniform, not to have to go through this rigmarole or to have to explain yourself at all.

Miracles, he would feel like saying, you're talking about miracles. Magic yes, miracles no. Miracles are for miracle-workers.

He never mentioned the word wizardry.

Now this pestering figure—there was none actually sitting beside him and he was free to just look out of the window—seemed to have become an agent of retribution lodged inside his head. Perhaps it was even his own mother, scornfully taking him to task.

So come on then, Mr Magician. Show us what you can do.

And, as it turned out, he was too late anyway. Even such powers as he might have applied, even the simple power of his presence, had miserably failed. He arrived to be told that his mother had passed away some two hours before—while he was still in fact on the train, having all those beside-the-point thoughts.

His mother was dead, gone, no longer there. Which left, apparently, an even greater challenge.

'But of course,' he was told, 'you can still see her if you wish ...'

See her? But how could he see her if she was no longer there? But then again, when the thing was put to him, how could he not? How could he have said, 'No thanks,' and turned around?

'Yes, I would like to see her. Yes.'

And there she was. And wasn't. There was a small quiet room in which his mother had been deposited and arranged. He was seeing her and he was not seeing her, though he could not beat back an even more bewildering possibility. Was *she* seeing him? Even judging him? Even delivering upon him her last judgement, her last unanswerable taunt.

So there you are, Ronnie. At last. Well thanks for coming anyway. What a pity we couldn't have had a last little chat. Perhaps it wouldn't have got us very far anyway, probably not. And in any case here's the main item for you. Here I am. Here we are. This is your mother, Agnes. And here's a fine little trick for you to perform, if you're up for it. So come on.

What could he do? Say things to her? The little room, with its curious drapery, had the effect of something pointedly, elaborately staged. Say he was sorry? Say he was sorry for everything, everything he'd done or not done. He seemed suddenly to grasp in his very flesh—then the comprehension deserted him—the most simple yet ungraspable of truths. This was his mother and he would not—could not—be here, standing here, were it not for her. This was his mother, yet she had vanished. Yet she was still here. How could anyone, anything, just vanish?

He bent to kiss her forehead. It was cold to his lips and she made no sign—no smile or frown or flinch—that she knew what he was doing. And he felt that his lips were touching also the cold surface of the water, the deep heedless water under which his father lay, unknowing too.

He had to stay another two nights to sort out some immediate things. It had been her heart, yes, her heart. She was only forty-nine. He might have chosen to sleep in the house in Bethnal Green, but he slept in the old flat in Finsbury—he had kept it on—where he and Evie had often slept together. He was both intensely glad that Evie wasn't there now and intensely conscious of her absence. It seemed an age since he and she had gone back that first time from the Belmont Theatre and she had asked him—at such a time—about his mother.

He had to go anyway, for practical reasons, to the house in Bethnal Green. He felt, while he was in it, in the house where his own life had begun and where his earliest memories had formed, like an intruder, an imposter, a thief.

These were two of the worst days of his life, but worse was to come. Did he have any inkling of it?

At Victoria Station, on his return, he saw that the Brighton platform was crowded with cheerful trippers heading for the coast, and he did a rare thing. He bought a first-class ticket, so that he could sit in shielded repose and gaze again out of the window. He heard his mother's voice distinctly. 'You come to see your dead mother, Ronnie, and you get a first-class ticket on the way back!' He was leaving her again. It was the right way round this time, or, more profoundly, the wrong way. He was going to Evergrene again with a label round his neck. No he wasn't.

As he sped back towards Brighton he found himself taking stock of his life almost as if it too might be over. This was preposterous, he knew. His life was all ahead of him. In a few weeks' time he would be marrying Evie. Yet in the space of little more than a year he had been twice visited by death. Once—with its blessing, its gift—in the form of Eric Lawrence. Now, with its condemnation, in the form of his mother. He was the complete orphan. He had lost even his foster-father, his mentor, with no final words of wisdom to help him. Truly, to believe in magic, let alone make it your occupation, you had to be a little mad.

Yet he still wanted to perform wonders, things that people would not believe.

His life was all ahead of him? Well, perhaps. His mother had been only forty-nine. His father, poor man, torpedoed by a German submarine, had been only thirty.

Parrots are supposed to have very long lives, but they are just birds. And they fly away.

As he peered through his first-class window, his nose pressed to the glass (no one would have seen his face), his eyes had filled with tears, yet at the same time he had asked himself a legitimate question: but aren't you happy? Didn't he have every reason to be happy? Hadn't he found in his still short life his purpose in it? Hadn't he found the woman he loved? Hadn't he had once a happy childhood, a wonderful unexpected second childhood? Perhaps his mother had always known.

People didn't like to say they were happy because they thought that then something bad might happen. But something bad *had* happened, so he was in the clear.

Though how could he say he was happy, even if he was, when his mother had just died? 'You come to see your dead mother, Ronnie, and then you go away and travel first-class and say you are happy!'

People didn't like to believe in magic and yet they could be so superstitious.

Outside, the suburbs gave way to green fields, Surrey became Sussex. Fields of wheat passed by, yellowed and glossy, waiting for the cut. But, sadly for the harvesters and for the holidaymakers packing this train, the sky was not the blue and benign one of his outward journey. Thick clouds had built up as they so often do in an English summer, and suddenly everything, flashing past him as it was, became tempestuous and dramatic. Rain lashed his window, the greenery before him became awash and blurred, so that his own watering eyes seemed silly.

But then, just as suddenly, while in one part of the sky rain kept falling, gleaming needles against still-dark clouds, half the world was full of sunshine again.

One evening at Evergrene, when he'd just turned ten, he had stood in the sitting room before Eric and Penny, who had positioned their armchairs next to each other. They were in a little row, he had an audience of two, and he stood facing them, the green-topped table beside him. He knew by now that the surface was called 'baize', a nice word, but he knew also that the table was not what it seemed. It was a table and not a table, and this might be true of a great many things. It was the first door that you had to pass through, as it were, into a new way of thinking about everything around you.

The table was just a table and it was plain to see that its green surface had nothing on it and that its legs were of the spindly collapsing kind that enabled the whole thing to be folded up and stored away. It was a card table, after all, only to be brought out when needed. But no one could see—because why should they?—that there were other foldings, closings and expandings involved in this table that were in the very space it occupied and around it. There was a whole other secret furniture available that it was the challenge to make any audience *not* see.

And, as Ronnie would later learn, what short-sighted fools they could be.

He tapped the table with his wand, then ran his hand several times across and around its surface. Then he tapped with his wand the spindly legs and waved the wand between them, all to show that the table was only a table and occupied nothing but air. He did these things with fluid unhurried movements—this was very important—making much play with his hands and arms. This was all to show that he was to be trusted, he was confident, he was in command—he was the performer here. But it was also to achieve certain other unseen things besides.

Then he walked round the table, first in one direction, then the other, circling it, again to show there was only air, but also to show that the table might in some way obey him, it was like a creature he had tamed.

His little audience of two would now be focusing on the table, regarding it inquisitively and keenly, and yet, unwittingly, being distracted in their very intentness in a way that he wanted them to be. Of course his audience, Eric and Penny, weren't like a real audience because they knew how the thing was done, but they were here to pretend that they didn't, and to see if he could do it and make even them not notice. It was a test, even you might say an audition. Eric felt that the time had arrived.

It was a simple task in the catalogue of magicianship. Make something appear on the table, something that hadn't been there a moment ago. What kind of object it might be is up to you. Surprise us. And remember: all the time make a *show*. Don't overdo it, but make a show.

It was dark outside, a late November evening, several weeks since Ronnie had been told that his father was 'missing', and he had almost got used to that fact by now. He had always been missing, after all. What was the difference? But there was a difference and Ronnie still struggled to understand it.

While he was hopeful on this evening that he could make something appear seemingly from nowhere—he had learnt how to do it—he knew he could not make his father appear. Or at least such a thing was not within his abilities yet, he was only an eager beginner. His recent intensified application to magic was itself, as Ronnie could only dimly see—but Eric and Penny could see it—a means of diverting attention, of distracting him from the pain of thinking about his father.

It was not one of Eric's 'warden' nights, but their own blackout curtains were meticulously in place, with the regular curtains closed before them. For all they knew, this might have been the night on which the Luftwaffe chose to shift its own attention from London or Liverpool to pulverise Oxford instead (in fact it was the turn of Coventry). But for the time being the sitting room at

Evergrene had turned into a little hushed theatre, the drawn curtains and just the light of two standard lamps, with their gold-fringed shades, adding to the mood.

Ronnie had thought about it carefully: *what* should appear on the table? His idea was perhaps not the most original one, yet it would do the work and enable him to add a special touch that might be more than just show-manly, and it had taken some preparing in advance.

Now, having done his circlings, he stood in front of the table and before Eric and Penny and extended his arms wide, palms flattened as if to confirm there was noth-ing—nothing—suspicious around him. Yet as he did this he felt a strange power. It was the power of this moment of performance, but he could not separate it from some thrilling capacity that he had actually acquired in himself and would always, from now on, simply *have*.

He felt too the strange power of his silence. He had not spoken a word and had not needed to—he had merely moved. And his silence seemed to have silenced his audience.

But now he made a sound that he'd never been intend-ing. Out it came spontaneously and forcefully, a sudden 'Hah!' or mere explosive gush of air from his lungs. At the same time he gave a flick of the wand—inertly lodged till now like an idle drumstick between two fingers—and brought his hands together above his head and clapped them. Then with a sweep of his arms and his whole body he stepped to one side.

On the table, at its centre, was a vase containing several large red roses. They were, as it happened, the last unwilted roses left on one of the bushes in the garden, surviving—perhaps because of some power Ernie had—well into November. Ronnie could see them from his bedroom window and as he pondered his forthcoming event they had suddenly called to him.

He had nonetheless thought it only right to seek Ernie's discreet permission. Ernie had said, 'All yours, Ronnie, ain't my roses.' He'd got the impression that Ernie somehow knew exactly what he was up to.

So, earlier this day, he had snipped off the best roses—five in all—and secreted them, as he'd secreted the vase.

And the result of it all was that Eric and Penny were now clapping energetically and even emitting the kind of squeals and gasps of delight that audiences generally, though Ronnie did not yet have the experience to know it, can emit. And he felt that their excitement was wholly genuine, they weren't putting it on, though they might easily have done, just for him.

It was his first taste of applause. Fucking 'ell.

But this was not all. Still with his suave and gliding movements and as if it were all part of the same act and perhaps, in its way, a kind of magic too, he took two roses from the vase and, stepping forward even as they continued clapping, presented one to Penny and one to Eric, in that order of course, with a little bow to each.

It had been a test, an audition, his first-ever performance, but he hoped that this final double gesture would have another meaning that though invisible—unlike, now, the vase of roses—they would yet 'see'.

As they took their roses they seemed quite overcome and he felt it again: there was no feeling like it. He had not merely done something that might be admired in an ordinary way, as a child might be admired for learning how to ride a bicycle. He'd done something quite out of the ordinary, even 'impossible', and the power to do it was with him. It was not just that a vase of flowers had appeared from nowhere. He himself had become a different person.

Jack had to make the announcement two nights running. 'Indisposed.' The groans of disappointment, even of disgruntlement, that this produced told him how much of a draw Pablo and Eve had now become.

'Yes, I know, I know,' he said. 'You'll just have to put up with more of me.'

He did not say of course why Ronnie (or Pablo) was 'indisposed'. He did not want to dampen their holiday mood further. And he did not answer the question, though it was not actually shouted out: 'What about Eve?' He extended his preceding act—'Silvery Moon'. He made a few more jokes. He said, 'You see, boys and girls, even magicians themselves sometimes have to disappear.'

'But don't you worry,' he said, 'he'll be back, Pablo will be back.' Which didn't, he knew, help those who'd bought tickets for that particular night. For some reason it came magnanimously into his mind that when Ronnie returned he should become the *Great* Pablo.

Improvising on the theme of moonlight, he threw in a whole extra soupy, though seasonal number: 'Shine On, Harvest Moon'. He'd negotiated unsuccessfully with the Rockabye Boys as to whether he might do an extra number with them (leather jacket, quiff and all: that would either show them up or send them up, he thought), but Doris Lane did condescend to allow him to perform a soft-shoe shuffle adoringly round her, provided *she* could do an extra number—'I've Got a Crush on You'. (It was like dancing round Queen Victoria and crush might have been the word, he was later reported to have said.)

At the end of the show he beefed up his farewell routine, giving added oomph—some might even have said surprising urgency—to 'Red, Red Robin'. *Live, love, laugh and be happy!* He did his best, all told, to make up for the sad gap in the evening's performance, but there were many—and who could blame them?—who simply felt that they hadn't got what they'd paid for.

To make matters worse, though it was hardly part of some malign conspiracy, the fine weather of the past few days broke and the pier was battered by heavy showers, the sea frothed. Which hardly eased audience dissatisfaction. But the seaside is like that: one moment gaiety and laughter, the next sodden misery.

A bit like show business.

And of course these were two nights when he could not have slipped back into the auditorium to cease to be Jack Robinson and become just a pair of eyes in the dark. Though on the other hand it was on the first of these two nights—and he didn't have to do it—that he confessed to Evie that this was just what, from time to time, he'd done. And even why.

Just an old song-and-dance man? But that wouldn't stop him, in the decades to come, having the long and distinguished career he would have, as an actor and then even as one of those who, off stage, put on, create the shows themselves. Just Jack Robinson, picking up girls whenever he liked? That usherette standing there. You never saw me, but why don't you come and see me after the show? But that didn't stop him, fortunately or unfortunately, from being a man who could fall in love. Or even from telling Evie White so.

'It wasn't the act I wanted to watch, Evie. It was you.'

And Evie, when she was suddenly but not so passively or helplessly on the receiving end of all this, could not help thinking: This is what he does, of course, with all of them. He makes them feel special, he makes them feel that they're the one. Hadn't she seen it happen enough times? And wasn't he now, blatantly, only seizing his opportunity? Ronnie was not there. The sheer obviousness of it all.

But she couldn't help feeling that she had a better measure of Jack than all the others, and that she had this same opportunity too. And why—it was a good, if uncomfortable question—hadn't she gone with Ronnie, to hold his hand, to see his mother, to be with him in his time of need? Be careful, she might have thought, you might just be Flora for the night. Though would that have been so awful, if nobody knew? It might even have been the better (or less bad) thing.

Yet she couldn't help feeling either—and this was the real push and dare of it—that she might really be the special one for Jack. If what he was saying to her now, about slipping back into the auditorium, was true, then she wasn't just some passing thing he'd only noticed yesterday.

And, fortunately or unfortunately, it was true. And, fortunately or unfortunately, she was right.

And hadn't it turned out in the end, and for nearly fifty years, to be entirely fortunately?

She looks in her mirror now and sees herself as she was then. Hardly a slip of seventeen not knowing what she was doing, and an engagement ring winking on her finger.

Ronnie had phoned. He'd said, 'I was too late, Evie. She's gone.'

It was the voice, strangely, of a man who'd done something wrong, and was now awaiting his punishment.

'Oh I'm so sorry, my darling. You mustn't blame yourself. Do you want me to come and be with you?'

And these were all the right words, except she might have been with him in the first place. Then everything would have been different.

He said he would be okay. He said it might mean a couple of nights. There were things he had to do, sort out.

She said, 'Take care, my darling, I'll be thinking of you.'

And that same night, after Ronnie had phoned, after Ronnie's mother had died, after the show in which she didn't appear, she'd got into bed with Jack Robbins. She'd thought of her own mother, her sunhat and frock. One day there might have to be some explaining. Guess what, Mum.

In the dark they'd talked about mothers. Everyone has to have one. It was the topic of the day. How strange, her head now lay on Jack's chest, her fingers wandered over it.

And as soon as Ronnie had returned he'd looked into her face and he'd seen. She knew it. She even had the feeling he'd looked into her face before he'd left and known it then, somehow, impossibly, beforehand. And she might simply have said in the first place, 'I'm coming with you.'

He just looked into her face and she knew that he knew. He didn't say anything. Nor, of course, did she. And wasn't the important thing to be talking about his mother?

'I'm so sorry, my darling.'

She might have been saying it on either account.

She'd got into bed with Jack Robbins. She'd known what she was doing. She'd even known that sooner or later it was bound to happen, as Jack had known. As much as anything can be bound to happen in life.

It was a Friday night, and she got to know Jack a lot more, even to know, a little bit, his mother, though she'd never met Jack's mother either. 'Mothers, Evie, who'd have 'em?' His chest rose and fell beneath her cheek. When she'd pressed her hand to the small of his back, he must have felt the prod of the ring against his spine. The weather had changed, but the storms kept away. All that night there were little blinks of light, just enough to make the curtains flicker for an instant, followed by low rumbles that never became louder, far out at sea.

But Ronnie did say one thing when he returned. He saw and he knew, and what he said, given that he knew, was close to what she might have expected him to say, but it was strange.

He said, 'I saw something, Evie.'

She waited a little, even prepared herself.

'You saw something?'

'Yes, I saw something. From the train.'

She looks in the mirror. Had her face, then, been so transparent? Not even like a face in a mirror, but like glass itself?

She could dance, she could smile, but she could never sing, and all her life she could never act either. No? She could not do that thing that all his life Jack could do—or so he'd make it seem—as easy as walking, as if for him it was no trouble at all to step out of himself, even to step through a mirror.

But then Jack had once said in one of his interviews—one of those moments of startling candour when you might have said he *wasn't* acting: 'Acting? We all do it, don't we? We all do it all the time.'

On the TV screen, she couldn't help noticing, his own face was showing its age.

This morning she'd done a strange thing. Anyone looking from one of the neighbouring houses in Albany Square might have thought it a weird performance. But then who would have been looking? It was very early. Which only made it weirder.

She'd woken and known at once what day it was, and what she must do. The thought and the deed were the same. She was wide awake, but she might have been sleep-walking. She got up and put on her dressing gown and, of all things, a pair of old trainers from the days when she used to do gym classes. She'd tied the dressing gown carefully round her and gone downstairs, through the quiet kitchen and into the garden. It was a still, clear morning, the sort that can mean an immaculate day to come, but it was not long after dawn and the low sun was only just creeping, dazzlingly, into the garden. The air was sharp and cold.

But she needed to do this thing that anyone watching would not even have been able to see. To carry with her, inside her dressing gown, the warmth of the bed—the bed where Jack had died one year ago—out to the place where, if he was anywhere, Jack was now. She must do it quickly before the warmth she was carrying was stolen from her.

But before she knew it, or saw it, she had stepped into the impossibly thin thread, slung between two shrubs, from which hung a complete spider's web. As she breasted the thread and as it stretched and then gave way, she saw for a second, from the corner of her eye, the intricate dew-silvered structure for which it had been spun, first in its agitated entirety, then in wilting collapse as it vanished into shadowed air. She had to flail with her arms to make sure she was not now enmeshed in its wreckage. And then she'd seen that the garden was dotted with the things, glistening and apparently hovering in the low shafts of sunlight.

It was the season for them, or for seeing them, and though a spider's web was one of the most familiar of mental pictures—who has not at some point doodled a spider's web?—the actuality was bewitching. How on earth was it done? How on earth were they conceived and constructed, these entrancing, lethal things?

She had not anticipated that the garden would be decked out like this, as if just for her. And look what she'd done. Intent on something else, she'd walked straight into one of these wonders and ruined it.

She'd thought, for an instant, of the silver tiara she used to wear, trapped above her fringe in her blonde hair.

Early September. Exactly fifty years ago the show had closed. The end of the season: the crowds departing, the light on the waves changing, the waves themselves, even in the way they gnawed at the beach, seeming to know something. Time to stack up the deckchairs and put them away.

September 1959: when she and Ronnie should have got married. Let's give it the season, let's give ourselves and the act the season. And wasn't their act, by that September—even by the middle of August—quite something, a success? What couldn't they do next?

There was something else Jack had said to her, when it all happened, when Ronnie was with his mum, or as it had turned out, not exactly with her. He'd said, 'Don't you think, Evie, that all this stuff, the pier, the show, the whole bag of tricks, it's had its day? It's not what they'll want for much longer. The future's elsewhere, don't you think?'

Only that last bit might have been part of some declaration to do with *them*. The rest was hard-nosed, if slightly sad. It was all a far cry from Jack Robinson, the man on the end of a pier, singing his song. It seemed she was with more than one person—two, three people—at the same time. And what might he have thought of her?

They were on the pier then, in that little reserved bit, and it was just the two of them. It was where, some weeks later, she dropped the ring. It was the morning after. The morning after he'd made the first announcement of the two announcements: 'Indisposed.' The morning after she hadn't had to perform—who did she have to perform with? But they'd gone off together, as she'd known they would, after the show.

And how had poor Ronnie slept, all alone, that night?

Yet what Jack was saying now didn't feel wrong at all, it felt shrewd. In her sharp little heart she could feel it was true. The weather had changed, but the storms had passed by and the sea, for the moment, was calm and sparkling. 'The whole bag of tricks', that's what he'd said. He had put his arm round her as if she was all his now, and she hadn't tried to remove it.

She'd got into bed with Jack Robbins one night in 1959 and the truth of it was that she'd never got out of it until a year ago. And she'd even, this morning, wanted to carry out to him the warmth of that same bed. It was all she could think of doing. She'd gone out into the garden, only to be ambushed by a network of shimmering gossamer. Her breath itself had glinted and swirled like silver dust in the cold air.

Exactly a year ago she'd woken up—from whatever dream she'd never remember though she might wish to be permanently back in it—and put out her arm. Jack was there, of course he was. But he wasn't. Something even in her fingertips had told her. He was there, but had gone. She didn't want to think about the seconds, the moments that had followed, yet every morning and every middle of the night she'd have to repeat this innocent, terrible act of waking up.

As if a year's worth of them would reprieve her now. As if, after all, he might really be there.

When she'd collected the ashes she'd dithered and wondered. Jack, ever helpful, had never said anything, had left nothing written down. She'd wanted anyway at first to have the pathetic feeling that she'd brought him back home to Albany Square. Perhaps she might just keep the ashes here with her in their jar, here in this bedroom. Under the bed. Better still, not even under. Perhaps she might just sleep with her husband's ashes. For several nights, she actually had. The things that we do.

Less than a year ago, one October morning, she'd done the simplest, most obvious thing—steeling herself to do it, all the same. She'd gone out into the garden and stood under the crab-apple tree that Jack, with much actorly ceremony, had planted as a sapling, and she'd scattered the ashes there. She hadn't offered much ceremony herself. It was not like the never-ending unendurable funeral. There was nobody else but her. She'd upturned the jar. It was all very simple, like applying some gardening product. And if they had to be scattered somewhere, then let it be close. The garden, of course.

And then, when it was too late, when she'd even thumped the bottom of the jar to get the last bits out, she'd had the thought: In the sea, in the sea, from the end of Brighton pier even. Was it Jack suddenly, mischievously intervening? Or someone else?

So what, then, might she have done today? She had a driver she could call at any time, Vijay, Jack's former driver, though really the company's driver. She might have said, 'Vijay, I'd like you to drive me to Brighton.' She might have sat in the back in stately silence, while Vijay, keeping understandingly silent too, just drove. She might have said when they got there, 'Give me half an hour, Vijay, then pick me up again here.' Then she might have strolled up and down the pier, where of course there was no longer any theatre, but there were still the railings and still that very spot. The ring, and then the ashes.

She might have leant for a while and looked at the waves and even whispered words. Then turned around and gone back to where Vijay was waiting. 'Okay, now drive me home please.'

Instead she'd stood in her dressing gown, like some batty old crone, seemingly speaking to a tree. The tree had looked down on her. Then she'd come inside, shivering, and got back into bed and sobbed like a punished child.

But it had been kind of George to remember, he was a considerate man. And how else would she have spent this whole day? So some time later she'd got up again, not a sobbing child but a seventy-five-year-old woman, and prepared herself slowly to meet George. She'd put on her face. The cream blouse, the straight black skirt, the little black jacket, the pearls. Her small clutch bag. She'd gone downstairs. It was twelve-thirty. She'd felt a little dizzy and strange, she'd felt a little not herself.

Then Vijay had called anyway, as arranged. He'd said, 'Good afternoon, Mrs Robbins.' She was really 'Evie' or 'Evie White' or 'Ms White', but she'd learnt—in almost fifty years—to accept the frequently conferred title without fuss. And perhaps today it was the right title, and perhaps Vijay meant it (did he remember?) in that way.

She'd smiled and confirmed the name of the restaurant. And twenty minutes later she'd followed the maître d' to the usual corner table, and there was George, rising from his seat as soon as he saw her.

'Princess, you look lovely as ever.'

She couldn't act?

'Princess'—at seventy-five? Only because Jack had always been the prince, or because (and George had better not forget it) she was controlling director of Rainbow Productions?

But this was not one of their business lunches. Polka-dotted silk had flopped from George's breast pocket as they sat. Two glasses of champagne were instantly poured. 'Well here's to him,' he had said.

Then, with the fish of the day—she couldn't afterwards remember which fish it was, but she'd definitely wanted fish—more glasses, of white burgundy. George had tasted, squeezed his lips and sagaciously approved. 'Bony but creamy,' he'd said.

For a moment she'd thought he'd meant her.

It was not a business lunch, but there was the ongoing issue of the biography, which George was not inclined to abandon. Several months ago she had said, 'Not on your nelly, George. Tell your literary-agent friend to go away.'

But perhaps in order to work round to it again, or just because of the nature of the day, he had got biographical anyway.

'So tell me, Evie—all these years and I've never really known. How did you and Jack, how did you first really . . .?'

He didn't know? Such innocence. For over thirty years Jack's agent? All those lunches with him. Wouldn't he have got the story anyway, or Jack's version of it? And now she was going to be put in the position of saying something that conflicted with it? Not on your nelly either, George. Did he think that because a year of her widowhood had respectfully passed, everything might now be up for grabs? He'd be saying next, 'So tell me, Evie, what happened, what really happened with that magician chap? I forget his name.'

She took a swallow of her wine. She was glad she had already done her sorrow and weeping, but she still might fall back, if needed, on excusing grief. The batty old woman in the garden and the bawling infant had turned into a princess sitting in a Mayfair restaurant, and now she was going to have to play her part, in honourable repayment of George's kindness, all through what might be a long and challenging lunch. It could hardly be a quick and casual one, given its purpose. And anyway she'd welcomed the means of passing the dreadful hours.

So she had performed her best. And after several glasses of burgundy she couldn't be sure what she had or hadn't said.

She had returned in the mellow sunlight of the waning afternoon. Vijay had actually touched his forehead. 'Have a good evening, Mrs Robbins.' So the house had entombed her again. Yet there was nowhere, for all the silenced voices, where she would rather be entombed. And the wine had done its work. Now she sat at her dressing table, wondering whether to remove her make-up and half expecting to see in the mirror Jack standing behind her, placing his hands softly on her shoulders.

'Exhausted, darling? That's George for you. I know how you feel. I'd take a little nap if I were you.'

But it wasn't Jack that she saw. It was too brief a glimpse for every detail, but he was in his stage outfit, the last thing she'd seen him in, and she'd recognise those eyes anywhere.

The show must go on. But must it? Who says? When are you allowed to say the show is over now, there's no more show any more? And anyway the show was always just what it was, a flickering summer concoction at the end of a pier. Jack had said it had had its day, it was all going out with the tide beneath them. He'd put his arm round her.

And in any case it must finish in September. And even in August, high season, you could feel it, the turning of the year, the shortening evenings, autumn lurking over the horizon. There comes a sad point in any holiday when you start to think: Only so much more of this left now, then back to the real world. But if you're in show business do you have to care about that? Isn't life a perpetual holiday? Up there on the stage isn't it all just a breeze, a doddle, a dream? Or that's what they all believe. Jack used to say, laughing it off, in interviews, 'One long holiday.' As if they thought there was no work in it. As if anyone could do it, get up there and do it.

But he was also known to say about his life in the theatre, and fortunately not in interviews, 'Fuck the real world. Who needs that?'

It was Evie who you might say chose to live in the real world, when she gave up the stage, where she'd disported and dazzled like the best of them, to become Jack Robbins' wife and, as it proved, rather more than that. What a big gamble that was, and what a big mistake it might have turned out to be. But look how it had paid off. Just look at her now. And all when she might have had her ongoing stage career, not to say marriage to Ronnie Deane, who had even become the 'Great Pablo'.

But who has heard of the Great Pablo now? That magician chap. Whatever became of him? And Jack never became the Great Jack, or even Sir Jack. But life is unfair, you do or you don't have your moment, and if the show must come to an end then there's always the sound theatrical argument: save the best till last.

Ronnie hadn't said anything. He'd just looked into Evie's eyes. Did it need a magician? And he saw that Evie saw that he saw. So what was to be said or done? It was confession time? Accusation time? Or time to carry on in a state of pretence—merciless or merciful pretence, which one would it be?

He had been to see his mother, who'd been there and not there. There was in each dissembling situation that had faced him one after the other a feeling of the world's having revealed its underlying falsity, as if the two con-frontations might have been the same.

He might have turned the tables. He might have unmagicked the magic. He might have really stuck those swords through Evie, truly have sawn her in half. Or just let the thought of such an expedient turn every perform-ance into a possible execution. That scream—was it *real*?

But of course not. How could he have done this to Evie? And all that stuff with the swords and the saw and the boxes, he'd been wanting to dispense with it for some time. It was just toys. It was just kids' stuff. It was not real magic.

This was to be the time anyway—when everything was falling apart—when their act really took off and Ronnie Deane, otherwise known as Pablo, but now not just that, even acquired greatness. All in the space of a few summer weeks.

And what might Eric Lawrence, who in his unseen but crucial way had made it all happen, have thought? He might have smiled, and been a little rueful even as he smiled. He'd never been known as the Great Lorenzo.

And what might his mother have thought? Silly ques-tion. 'You come to see your dead mother, Ronnie, and then you go away and call yourself the Great Pablo!'

And Evie? Still just 'Eve', only 'Eve'. Wasn't that a kind of demotion, a punishment? No. Wouldn't 'Eve' always have its immaculate ring? First of women. And did the world need to be told, to have it confirmed, that for him she would always be the great Eve, the wonderful Eve. And, if only for a little while, *his* Eve.

'And now, folks, I want you to meet a friend of mine. I used to call him Pablo, but now I'm going to call him the Great Pablo. You heard what I said, folks, and I mean what I said and you'll see why in a moment. I want you to give a big hand to the Great Pablo! And I want you to give a big hand too—and I know some of you gents would be only too glad to—to the Great Pablo's one and only helper—the one and only, the delightful, the delicious, the delorable *Eve!*'

The moment would come. There would be a pause, a hush, a tingle. Even the audience would know it—'Come and See with Your Own Eyes!' Everything else had been a preliminary. This was the famous finale.

How many times, Evie thinks now, did they perform it in that last month or so? No more than thirty. But enough times for it to become legendary and spoken of, even to be named on the billboards. And each time—she could vouch for it—more amazing and (literally) more glowing than the last.

And how was it done? She would never tell, of course she wouldn't. And for a simple reason. She merely took part in it, she 'assisted'. She simply did what he told her to do. Well she would, now, wouldn't she? What else could she do? She had her legs, her famous legs, but she no longer had a leg to stand on.

Ronnie would have the lights dimmed. He was the Great Pablo, so could command such things. Only dimmed and only briefly. Illusions, he was known to say, should always be done in good clear light, otherwise people might suspect it was all just—trickery.

The dimness was just a signal, an anticipation. You might hear a general whisper. Then down in the pit the drummer (he was called Arthur Higgs) would start his own little whispery scuffling. A little gathering shimmer on the cymbals. Then the lights would come up. They were seeing only what they were seeing.

From the wings Ronnie would bring the small round table and place it centre stage, and she would bring the glass of water and—with the customary lift of her knee and flurry of her feathers—place it on the table. Then she would step—pirouette—to one side. It was her role now simply to watch, and the audience might watch him or they might watch her, it was their choice, but in a little while they would be watching neither him nor her, but something, you might say, using the exact word for the situation, that transcended both of them, even, you might say, transcended them all.

He would pick up the glass of water and take a sip, just to show that it was only that, a simple tumbler of water. He would put it back on the table. He would pull from his breast pocket his big white shiny handkerchief. Nothing unusual so far. He would give the audience one of his stares. You think so, you think so—nothing unusual? Then he would drape the handkerchief over the glass and you'd see the handkerchief move, twitch by itself. That was because the glass had turned into a white dove.

Not so unusual either (though try it yourself).

Then he'd lift off the handkerchief, pick up the dove, let it perch for a moment on his fingers before tossing it, fluttering, over the heads of the audience. And it would be gone. It would not be there. How? Had they really seen it in the first place?

But all this was nothing.

He would take the white handkerchief and hold it by the corners between his hands and pass it in front of the table (it was such slick actions that made Evie think of a toreador) and then there would be the glass of water again. He would pick it up and drink, all of it this time, then put the glass back on the table.

Then it would seem that something was nudging, struggling inside his mouth, trying to get out. He'd pull at it. Something white. The white dove? Surely not. The white handkerchief? No, that was back in his pocket. It was the end of a white rope, a thin white rope, just the start. He'd pull out a bit more. Then some more. That's when she would stop watching and step forward—not without pausing to cock a knee and shake her plumes—and take the end of the rope and carry on the pulling.

Or rather she didn't pull so much as walk backwards across the stage—some stops again to shimmy and smile as if she knew something the audience didn't—holding the end of the rope while it still kept coming, more and more, out of Ronnie's mouth, while Ronnie himself stepped back to his side of the stage as if to make room for this white tongue of rope.

Evie might have said to him, while they were

rehearsing—but 'rehearsing' by those days was hardly the right word—'Bloody hell, Ronnie, how do you get so much rope in your mouth?' But did she dare ask any such silly questions now?

The strange thing was that the rope wasn't wet or slimy, it was a soft silky thin white rope, white as her own name was Evie White. She would remember the look and the feel of it even half a century later as she sat at a dressing table removing a pearl necklace, letting it slither over her fingers. And the strange thing was that it was like so many things that appeared now in their act. She never saw where they had been beforehand, where they were kept. They just appeared. Like the white dove. Or was there more than one of them? Was there a new one every night?

But the white dove was nothing.

With his mouth full of rope, Ronnie could hardly have answered that question of hers anyway. He just made a gesture with his eyes that she should keep on pulling and walking. It was what he said in any case before they started rehearsing. 'All you have to do is pull and walk away.' It seemed like some strange surrendering statement of fact, not just an instruction, so that when she started pulling and the rope just kept coming she had the peculiar and uncomfortable feeling that she was pulling the very stuffing, the very life out of him, and he was letting her do it.

Well, she had let him saw her in half.

All you have to do, Evie, is just pull and walk away. So, every night, she just kept on pulling.

Down in the pit, as the rope kept coming, the drummer would have started up again, with a slow crescendo, his wait-and-see whisking and thrumming. Ronnie would be on the other side of the stage and there would be a stage-width of rope between them before Ronnie finally took his end (so it had an end) out of his mouth and held it. Then a strange thing would happen. They'd each hold their end of the rope and start to swing it forward and back, and then to whirl it round and round, faster and faster, like an enormous skipping rope. And the drummer would be doing his stuff, louder and louder. And then—

Then the rope would just disappear, it wouldn't be there any more, but between them, arching between them, there would be a rainbow. A rainbow, there wasn't anything else to call it. Stretching right across the stage: a rainbow. The drummer would have stopped, as if himself struck dumb. You could hear the silence, the sound of amazement. And then from somewhere out of the back of the stage would come—was it? Yes it was—the white dove, flying under the rainbow, and it would land on the rim of the glass, looking a bit dazed and as if it could do with a drink. Then there would be a big drum crash (Ronnie must have had a word with Arthur, he must have bought him a pint or two) and all would go black. No rainbow. End of act.

Except for the bows of course, when the lights came up again—Ronnie standing still and just solemnly dipping his head, but she'd be scissoring with her knees and throwing up her white-gloved arms and generally prancing and cavorting round him and egging the audience on in their applause, as if he really might be the Wizard of Oz.

And perhaps he was.

Was there ever applause like it—they had all seen a *rainbow*—and could there ever have been such a heralding of a career, a life in magic?

Top billing. And for those last two or three weeks the billboards actually said, 'Come and See the Famous Rainbow Trick!' Ronnie let the word 'trick' pass. It was the common word. And did he, really, have anything to complain about?

And don't ask her, don't ask Evie White. Though she if anyone, apart from Ronnie himself, should have known.

Even Jack had said, 'Surely *you* must know. A fucking rainbow right across the stage. How the bloody hell does he do that?' But she had shaken her head and might even have looked a little shifty and cornered as if she were being forced into some kind of betrayal. Betrayal? What betrayal? And perhaps they'd both looked a bit shabby and edgy and ashamed. Outdone, outshone by a rainbow.

But it wasn't even the best trick of all. That was still to come.

'So tell me, Evie . . .' George had begun.

Anyone can say they don't know, profess ignorance, or, after fifty years, simply say they don't remember. Not that George was exactly interrogating her. Or he was a sly and gentle interrogator, who'd always had, she suspected, a soft spot for her. He poured more wine. 'All your secrets are safe with me, you know that.' A reassuring statement if ever there was one, coming from Jack's 'wily' agent. Did she 'know' it? And 'all'? She could see that this lunch was going to require some negotiating.

How old was George? Sixty-eight, sixty-nine? A soft

spot? Come off it. He was just trying to soften her up. Bony but creamy. He surely didn't think that because her year of mourning was now over—

But it was all suddenly a little like that treacherous and bewildering period long ago, when she was with Ronnie, yet not with him, and yet felt loyal. When she was with Jack, yet not with him, and yet would be with him—though she didn't know it—for most of the next fifty years. How might the matter be solved?

But the matter *was* solved, for them all. Ronnie solved it.

Secrets. Who doesn't have them? And are they ever safe? Even with ourselves?

'The Life and Times of Jack Robbins'. No, not if she could help it. Over my dead body, George. Though what was there to hide? The story of a successful career and a successful marriage, how boring was that?

'But how about,' she might have said to George—a cunning, yet risky diversionary tactic—'"The Life and Times of Ronnie Deane"?'

'Who, Evie?'

'You know—that "magician chap". Otherwise known as the Great Pablo. You don't know? Did Jack never tell you?' Staring at George over her wine glass.

Or, she thinks now, staring into her mirror, 'The Life

and Death of Ronnie Deane'. If death was the word. Hadn't she just seen him, in this mirror? If 'death' was ever the right word. And 'gone' or 'missing' or 'not there', these were all, she knew by now, preferable words. Preferable, if more painful.

Or how about—her mind raced, as if she might have proposed to George that she would write it herself and start work immediately—'A Season in Brighton'? But no, she knew a better title. A mysterious title, but a better one, the best one. What was the name again, George, of that literary-agent friend of yours? That literary-agent chap. Wouldn't he like a nice mystery story? Called 'Evergrene'.

She thought of that impossible thread, stretched across the garden, so thin as to be almost not there, yet for a moment resisting, clutching her blundering body. She thought of that white rope stretched across the stage.

How much had Ronnie ever told Jack? Whatever it might have been, it had gone a year ago with Jack. She was the only true guardian now of the life and times of Ronnie Deane. The one always best equipped to tell the tale. Or to keep it to herself.

How often had she and Jack talked about Ronnie? Not much. A mutual silence about him, a guilty baffled honouring silence, was almost one of the glues—the secrets as they say—of their marriage. And, after all, how did they really know that he wasn't still *there*? She never told Jack what she'd done with the ring. Though he would have seen that it was suddenly absent. He didn't ask. He might have guessed. She hadn't given it back to Ronnie. Ronnie hadn't asked for it back. In fact she wore it for those last shows—for that very last show—as if it were a vital part of their act. A last little piece of shiny magic.

But then, after everything else had happened, she threw it into the sea. What else? She wept as she threw it. End of story. And yet she'd been seized, even as she threw it, by some crazy idea, some old fond belief she'd read about somewhere, that if you threw something precious into the sea it would bring something back to you.

She'd said it, into the wind, as if he might actually be out there somewhere: 'Ronnie.'

She says it now, into the mirror. 'Ronnie.'

And Jack never knew, unless he'd been a sort of burglar in his own home, that she'd kept the little costume of sequins and feathers. It wasn't so difficult to put it away and hide it, once you'd taken it to pieces, once you'd removed the plumes from where they fitted. There wasn't so much of it, really. And the tiara too, with its own white plume. And the long white gloves. They were all folded up together and carefully wrapped in tissue paper and kept somewhere locked and safe.

Now they were in the bottom drawer on the right-hand side of the dressing table where she was sitting. In all these years (she assumed) Jack had never known she still had the costume. Though once, long years ago, he'd slipped into the auditorium secretly, just to watch her wearing it.

But in fifty years she had hardly ever looked at it either. So what had she kept it for and why shouldn't she have shared with Jack the fact that she still had it? Why keep a secret that's almost a secret from yourself? She had sometimes thought if she opened the drawer she might discover the costume had gone.

Since Jack died she'd got it out several times. It was somehow a comfort, a need. She'd laid it out on the bed, she'd brushed it and combed the ostrich plumes and clipped them back in place. And had she—? Had she ever?

Well, that *would* be telling. And, anyway, how absurd.

It was the original outfit—the one she'd worn just for Ronnie at the Belmont Theatre. When, thanks to Jack, they got the Brighton season, she'd had a second one made, almost identical, so she'd always have the change right through that summer. And she'd kept the original all these years, and never told Jack. Though Jack must have seen her in one or the other of those outfits—how many times?

And she'd never told Jack about something else, though it had weighed upon her. It was much heavier in fact than a little made-of-nothing costume wrapped up in tissue paper.

It was February 1960. They'd got married in Camden Registry Office, back in London. The Brighton thing— the 'investigation'—had died down by then, though could it ever, exactly, go away? Any day there might be—news.

But she was Mrs Robbins now, though she preferred to be known as plain Evie White. And Jack was Jack Robbins, as opposed to Jack Robinson. He would never be that phantom figure again. If Ronnie had gone out of their lives, then so too had Jack Robinson. Where was he? Who was he? Where had he gone?

There might, she thinks now, be another story, another racy little book. 'The Life and Times of Jack Robinson'. Best told of course by Jack himself—or by a string of girls? Each one of them with a little chapter of her own. Or, no, just a paragraph. And each one of them with the same name.

It was 1960. Jack had been right, it was all going out with the tide, and who'd want that stuff any more when they could get it anyway from a box in the corner of their living rooms? And yet for a little while the 1960s were much like the 1950s. And what did that little box still trade in? *Sunday Night at the London Palladium*—with always a compere who'd become the nation's pal and always some magician and always some troupe of bouncing leg-waving smiling girls—well, it would seem to go on for ever. So where was this boat then that they might have been missing?

'Did Ronnie ever tell you, Jack, about a place called Evergrene?'

There. She had said it.

'Evergrene? No, Evie. Where the hell's Evergrene?'

'It's a house. It's the name of a house. Where he got sent in the war.'

'No, I never heard him say anything about Evergrene.'

'The Lawrences? Eric and Penny? They lived there.'

'Ah. The sorcerer's apprenticeship, you mean? The Wizard? That's what he called him, you know. Seriously. I never knew his name was Eric. But I think he was still in touch. I think he was still even going to see him.'

'Eric Lawrence died, nearly two years ago now.'

'Ah. I didn't know that.'

'But I've been wondering.'

'Wondering what?'

'Do you think that's where Ronnie went? Do you think he might be there?'

'Where?'

'Evergrene.'

Jack never took it any further. Why should he? He had his own reasons for forgetting his old friend Ronnie Deane. Let alone for not wanting to know if he might still be alive. They were Jack and Evie now. He had even given her a strange searching look. How much of this nonsense was she going to keep up?

She, too, had her reasons not to take it any further. Though was her mad theory (hope?) so mad? She hadn't gone with Ronnie to see his mother. It was no secret now where that had led. But suppose she *had* gone.

She might even now, but in some place other than Albany Square, be guarding, keeping scrupulously dusted in its glass case, the career of the Great Pablo. But perhaps he would have dispensed with the ridiculous name. As he would have dispensed eventually, even at her own sensible suggestion, with his glittering stage partner, Eve. Though not with his partner for life, even manager for life. He might have got his own TV magic show. But anyway done astonishing things that made people gasp and kept up the tradition of magicianship, of there being such a thing as magic in the world.

But she hadn't gone with him and things had turned out as they had.

And, as it also turned out, she could never have met, either, Ronnie's other 'second' mother, as Ronnie himself might have thought of her: Mrs Lawrence, Penny Lawrence.

She should go there herself. She had dithered and doubted. But didn't she have a sort of obligation? And if her intuition should prove correct? She should go and see this woman and so make up in some way for her own lapses and omissions. This woman who was the widow of the man—the wizard—who had taught Ronnie about magic and even enabled him (by nothing more magical than a bequest in his will) to find his 'Eve'.

She should honour the ghost of this man. And she should talk to Mrs Lawrence and even ask her—though would it even be necessary to ask her?—where Ronnie was now.

But she was too late.


Among the items left to Ronnie after Eric Lawrence's death and thus among the items left by Ronnie were a few solicitors' letters. It was not so difficult to phone up the office in Oxford, pretending to be a distant relative.

'I'm sorry to say Mrs Lawrence is no longer alive. She died last year. Yes, that's right, it was not very long after Mr Lawrence died.'

And the house?

'Evergrene? Yes, that's right. It's on the market now. It was put up for sale by Mrs Lawrence's brother—he lives in Canada—not so long ago.'

She'd hesitated once more. Canada? Should she simply draw the line there? But one day, when Jack was to be busy with rehearsals, she seized her opportunity. A train from Paddington.

The estate agent had said he could drive her out there, it wasn't so far. She had to spend an hour or so in the company of an over-attentive young man, clearly pleased to be out of the office and to be showing her what he called 'quite a posh' house. He might have wondered why she was so interested in this particular property and, assessing her age and possible bank balance, had his doubts. But—she couldn't act? And in any case a wedding ring (what a useful little accessory) now shone on her finger.

It still shines on her finger, embedded in its wrinkles, now. And how many times has she touched it today?

It wasn't that posh at all, even in her own lowly judgement. It was all a strange, rather bleak disappointment. Why had she come? To destroy the image she could, now, no longer carry in her mind? It was just an Edwardian house at one end of a straggly village. The village seemed to have undergone much post-war development and become almost a suburb of Oxford. It was not a long car ride. The house was not in the depths of the country nor in splendid isolation. It was a largish house with gardens front and back, but not particularly distinctive and fairly run-down. There was nothing to suggest the mansion full of wonders that Ronnie had seemed to evoke whenever she'd got him, sometimes with much effort, to speak of it.

It was perhaps necessary to jump back somehow more than twenty years and place herself in the mind of an eight-year-old boy from Bethnal Green. But how did you do that?

It was March, the thin end of winter, and the place even looked rather grim. You would have said, very readily, that it had no magic. It had been thoroughly cleared, and inside it was drab and echoey. Floorboards creaked. She didn't need a separate tour of the muddy and overgrown back garden. She could see it clearly from one of the upper windows. A small greenhouse and a cold frame, both with smashed glass. Beside the house there was a tumbledown wooden structure that hardly merited the description 'garage'.

All the while she had to keep up her performance with the pressing young man. So what line was her husband in then? It was hard to get away from him, to find even a moment of contemplation, but she'd done her best. No house could have looked more gloomily empty, but she said it, and said it, necessarily, inside her head: 'Ronnie? Are you still here?'

As her back was turned to the young man, as she looked from the window, she had felt a stab, her eyes had started with tears. Evie White. Since when had she deserved her spotless name?

But she could always say, at least to herself, that she had been there. She had done it. What more could she do? And, yes, engraved in the stone archway over the front porch, amid other decorative work—oak leaves, flowers, scrolls—was the name that must once, and for some unknown reason, have been confidently chosen and then sharply chiselled, but was now blotched and eroded by a dark-greenish mould: EVERGRENE.

She never told Jack she had gone there. It was another half-century secret. And was it still there now? And who was living in it?

18 Albany Square was still here—just about, it suddenly seemed to her. And who was living in it? As she looked in her mirror, this suddenly seemed a question you could ask too.


Penny Lawrence, having taken out the mug of tea and the glass of ginger beer, quickly made herself scarce. She knew by now when to vanish and when to appear. She was as good at it as those rabbits, though goodness knows how they knew what to do, when to be there or not, it was beyond her. They were about to appear now, she was sure of it. Eric had that look about him.

She had delivered the two drinks and then said, as was her way, but perhaps particularly brightly, 'Here we are!'

Once, years ago, when the two of them were what was known as 'courting', he had asked her, one summer evening, to come and see his dad's allotment in Cowley. His dad was somewhere playing cricket. He'd said there might be some spare runner beans she could have for her mum. It wasn't the most romantic of invitations, but the allotment included a shed and she'd thought: Aye aye. But he'd done nothing more bold, at first, than to fetch out two fold-up wooden chairs, like you see in church halls.

It was a nice evening, there were swallows flying about, and it was as though they were sitting in front of their own little house. She was nineteen. It was 1916. They were lucky, the war would miss them both. His father was a manager at the Morris works and so had found him a job there too, in the office, when it had mainly gone over to arms contracts. This had probably saved him.

Eric Lawrence, for the time being, was a bookkeeping clerk, very familiar with double-entry and the cost of hand grenades, but he said that when the war was over he wanted to do something different with his life. Quite different.

Then he said, 'Look behind you, Penny.'

Bloody hell. And how on earth?

Then he said, 'Now look again.'

Later he said it was his 'magic shed'. In more ways than one. She got the strong impression that evening that Eric and his father might indeed have very different outlooks. Though Eric's father had probably saved Eric's life. And just as well.

And now he was about to play the same trick on Ronnie. She felt an odd twinge of jealousy, but it was mixed up with a secret excitement, even with a sudden flood of happiness. It was time. This little Ronnie of theirs (of theirs?) was about to be introduced.

Play the trick? No, *do* the trick. Not even trick. Eric's word was 'illusion'.

And of all the things. Other young men might have put on other shows, gone to other lengths (some young men even drove cars—Eric's father, naturally, drove a Bullnose Morris) to woo a young woman. Or they might have just got on with it. But Eric had asked her one July evening to an allotment, with a promise of a bag of beans. And it had worked. It had done the trick.

Later, she'd had the strange thought that if he could do such things, then why hadn't he just magicked her into compliance in the first place? Why the beans, why the rabbits? But then perhaps he had. How did she know that her whole life with Eric wasn't some kind of hypnosis?

And 'their Ronnie'? Why couldn't Eric have found some magic, long ago, to solve their little problem? Though, true, it was more her little problem. But now, twenty-odd years later, and better late than never, they had Ronnie.

Eric had one day turned into Lorenzo (whatever next?) and now Eric, or Lorenzo, had almost stopped doing his stage work because of the war. Magicians weren't wanted in a war. You'd think they might be needed all the more. But he clearly hadn't stopped altogether. They don't stop, or retire, or even give it a rest. It was a thing for life. And she'd long ago come to appreciate that nothing was surprising. Nothing.

He'd signed up as an air-raid warden, so as to do his bit. Magicians can be air-raid wardens too. And there was already talk going around (which turned out to be not so silly) that the Germans were never going to touch Oxford, even with the Cowley works close by.

Every other night he went out after dark with his helmet and his whistle—and his wand?

She sometimes fancied she could write a book: 'I Married a Magician'. It might be interesting for some people, it might shed some light. But of course she'd never write such a book, because it would involve telling, and you could never tell. It was forbidden. Her part in it all, even her part now with the rabbits and the cold frame, you'd never get it from her. Though one thing she might say—it was a different sort of telling—was that it could all get very demanding. What about normal life?

But it could also get exciting. It could even get wonderful.

She watched Eric talking. She watched Ronnie's dark little head turn. There we are! There we go! Her heart went out to him—even more than usual. She knew he had his real mother, called Agnes, but she wasn't here to see or know, was she?

And normal life? What was that anyway? Here they were in another war, the second of their lives. It was going on right now, though, looking at this scene before her, you'd never know. And yet it was the whole point with this young guest of theirs (she didn't like to dwell on it): if it wasn't for a war.

She had an older brother, Roy, in Canada, who'd done well for himself and never ceased to remind her of it, and had two boys, one of them coming up to eighteen. Well, Canada was in this war too. And this little Ronnie's father, it seemed, was out there on a ship somewhere (she didn't like to think about this either) bringing in supplies—quite possibly from Canada.

Roy had always scoffed that if she'd married a magician she could have anything she liked, couldn't she? She only had to say. But at twenty-one she'd had a nasty miscarriage which had wrecked her chances of ever having babies again and there was no magic, it seemed, that could put that right. Though shouldn't she be glad now not to have a young boy or two coming up to eighteen?

There was no magic for some things, it seemed. It couldn't stop wars, and though it was a selfish, even a wicked thought to have, she couldn't help being glad about that now. Producing white rabbits out of nowhere was certainly something, but it was nothing compared with this little Ronnie Deane who'd turned up so late in the day.

So let them keep on fighting, that was her secret thought. And what war anyway? She couldn't see one.

Ronnie's mum had sent him to the best place, all right, even if she didn't know it and it had all just been the luck of the draw. She'd sent him to the best place, as far as she, Penny Lawrence, was concerned.

She saw his head turn back again and she knew his eyes would be wide and wondering now. He had beautiful dark eyes too, enough to melt your heart.

It had started to be called the 'Rainbow Trick', even the 'Famous Rainbow Trick', and God knows how it was done. But it wasn't, even so, the biggest trick of all. That was saved for the last night, the last show of the season, Saturday 12th September.

Ronnie had said before they went on, 'It's the last night, Evie, so let's give it a bit of extra whirl.' His eyes had never looked at her—or looked through her—so intently. And, yes, they'd given the rope some extra whirl. She could feel Ronnie, at the other end, through the rope itself, urging her, insisting. More, more! Faster, faster! And when it had appeared—there was always that gasp when it appeared—the rainbow had glowed even more brightly, every colour in it had shone more distinctly, and it had remained visible just a bit longer before disappearing. It was always like a real rainbow in that respect, it would just suddenly appear, then just as suddenly vanish.

But that night, and only that night, there was something else different—or new altogether. Unless it was all imagined. Though how could it have been imagined, if people agreed that they had clearly seen it?

But Ronnie, beforehand, had given her no warning, he'd said nothing.

It wasn't a white dove that flew out from under the rainbow and landed on the empty tumbler. It was something that looked at first almost like some broken-off whirring piece of the rainbow itself. It had feathers of all colours, blue and red and yellow, but mainly a vivid brilliant green.

It was a parrot.

Drum crash, darkness. More gasps. Cries even. Then the lights came back on again, for their bow, their final bow. A thundering of applause, and both of them looking this time a little dizzy and dazed, as if they'd astonished even themselves. And an extra touch, an extra twist, or mystery. Perched on Ronnie's lifted hand, on his knuckles, even as he took his bow, was the parrot.

So—they had really seen it. As they'd really seen the

rainbow. With his other hand he held hers, in traditional chivalrous bow-taking style, but now, as the applause roared on, he moved towards her, lifting her clutched wrist, and kissed it. Oh Ronnie could dance, their whole act was a dance. The parrot, which she'd never seen before, was still raised up on his other hand. Then he released hers and took the parrot and launched it out towards the audience like some bouquet that was theirs to catch. But it was gone. Gone.

As was Ronnie.

When did it happen? How did it happen? It was their last bow, but there was still Jack's goodnight routine to come. Though how could you follow such a thing?

It was the last show and it couldn't end without Jack Robinson's last farewell. There'd been talk too of some general final curtain call. So they should remain in costume just in case. For that reason she'd stayed with the rest of them in the wings, even as Jack came on. He brushed past her and said quickly in her ear, 'Jesus Christ, Evie—a fucking parrot!' Then when she looked round Ronnie was gone. Back to the dressing room, she supposed, to take a breather.

But no, he would never be seen again in the dressing room either.

She stayed in the wings to watch Jack, thinking Ronnie would rejoin her. On stage, Jack was giving his own last number a bit of extra whirl too, a bit of extra zing and punch. He was getting them all to join in. Even in the wings they were singing along (the voice of Doris Lane piercing through everyone else's).

*Wake up, wake up, you sleepy head!*

He was giving it his all.

*Get up, get up, get out of bed!*

But Ronnie was gone. Really gone.

He might have been sitting, exhausted, in the dressing room, wiping off his make-up. He'd given it his all too, hadn't he? Taken *his* final bow. And, yes—follow that. And he was the Great Pablo, wasn't he?

But no. He was nowhere to be found.

Everyone looked, of course they did. The whole theatre looked, the whole pier looked. The Brighton police began to look. In time it seemed that half of Brighton was looking. Enquiries were extended to London. His flat was broken into and searched, likewise his late mother's house. Jack, while Evie had to remain, went up to town to do some sombre searching of his own, taking with him a list of theatres, headed by the Belmont.

But nothing. Ronnie Deane had not been seen and was nowhere to be found. The most puzzling thing, for some, was that nor was his outfit—the red-lined cape, the white gloves and so on—nor were his personal magical bits and bobs, his actual bag of tricks. It was an ordinary brown-leather holdall, but contained such things as a wand, a string of special handkerchiefs, a large shiny key. And a white rope?

None of these things was found, nor the holdall itself. Nor any doves. Nor a parrot.

The police wanted to know—and naturally she came in for the closest questioning—about the parrot. They had not been at the show themselves and were inclined to disbelieve it all. A parrot? A *rainbow*? Being the police, they were professionally inclined to disbelieve anything they couldn't see, so to speak, with their own eyes. On the other hand, they had to deal with what they were told.

A parrot? But it was usually a dove? So where did he keep them then, the parrots and the doves? Where were they now? Perhaps because they had so little other evidence, they seemed to become quite compelled by this line of questioning, as if, despite themselves, their inquiry had shifted to one into the nature of magic—or rather into the exposure of its fraudulence. Magic, in fact, might be the culprit they were looking for. And Evie had found herself coming in for the kind of interrogation that she'd only previously envisaged in some dark recess of her mind.

Was this then her punishment? Punishment or test?

So how did he do all these things, they had said. How were they done? When she said she really didn't know, it seemed only to place her under increasing suspicion. Didn't know, or was just trying to hide something? They looked at the ring on her finger. They looked, it seemed, into her deepest motivations. For a while at least, it seemed that the police suspected they might be being elaborately fooled. Or tricked.

But there's a point where a trick ceases to be a mere trick. It was all a gift, of course, for the local, then even the national press. 'Magician Vanishes'. 'Seaside Sorcerer's Mystery Disappearing Act'. But it was not a matter for cheap humour. And there was the inevitable if distressing and unwanted thought: The sea. The sea itself. The end of the pier? He'd jumped?

Jack had once jokingly said, when the show opened,

'And if things get really bad, playmates, we can always all take a running jump. You can't do that at the fucking Hackney Empire either.'

They searched. There were police boats, divers. The seaside generally and not just Brighton can be prone to those incidents when someone, it unaccountably seems, simply 'takes to the water' to be seen no more. A little pile of clothes, perhaps, left on the shingle. But surely a red-lined cloak and other such garments would not have been hard to spot lying on Brighton beach. And surely a man wandering round the streets in such attire, and carrying a brown-leather holdall, could not have got very far.

He'd just disappeared. He was never seen again. It's a magician's prerogative and ultimate recourse perhaps.

'And you really can't think, Miss White, you're absolutely sure, of any reason why . . .?'

No, she couldn't. No. Didn't know or just wasn't telling? And to Jack she had to say the same thing, though in a different and more agonised way, 'Don't ask me, don't ask me. How should I know?'

Which is just what she might have said to Ronnie when he came back that day from seeing his dead mother, when he'd looked into her eyes and she'd known what he'd seen there. 'Don't ask me, Ronnie, don't ask me.'

He was never found, he'd just disappeared. Which meant of course that no one actually knew. Or ever would. He was like his own poor father who was only ever officially listed as missing. So, in theory . . .

Soon enough the police lost interest. There was no corpse, no crime. There was scarcely any evidence of anything at all. He was a grown man, not a lost child (and Brighton every summer had its fair share of those). To vanish was not illegal.

And it was not for the police, even while their investigations were intense, to note the simultaneous cooling off—though it was more like a jolt, a shakenness—in the relations of Evie White, Ronnie Dean's distressed assistant and fiancée, and Jack Robbins, compere of the show.

When Jack went up to London Evie knew it was as much to enable a contrite separation as anything else. They spoke on the phone, when they might have spoken in his bed, in his digs where once the lightning flashes had lit the curtains. When he phoned she thought of Ronnie's call from London barely a month before. Under police restriction, if not exactly under detention, she kept to her own digs, to the bed that had been hers and Ronnie's but was now just hers. How dreadful was that time. How dreadfully, decades later, it would loom in her memory.

Yet when the police wound up their inquiry and said she was free to travel, there she was again, and thankfully, in Jack's bed. Two final nights in Brighton, their fortnight's mutual avoidance like the quaint agreement of couples not to see each other on the eve of a wedding.

He would be seventy-eight now, Ronnie Deane. Or the Great Pablo. He might at any time just walk through the door.

But then she has had that same thought too, and too many times to count, about Jack. It's one of the temptations, the tortures of grief. Any moment now . . . But how could you bear it, live with it, without that teasing, rescuing illusion?

'You know, Evie,' George had said, 'I think he could just walk into this restaurant right now and sit right here at this table.'

Her eyes had sprung with tears. He saw at once it had been a big mistake to say it. He put a gentle hand on her wrist. Out from his breast pocket came the silk handkerchief.

'No, George, it's all right. I think it myself. All the bloody time.' She'd given a brave little laugh. 'Sometimes I think I can hear him say, "I fooled you all, didn't I?"'

And sometimes, she might have said to George, she'd thought he really *had* walked back into the house. Or someone had. She might have called out—perhaps she really had—quite simply and naturally and unalarmed, as if time had simply somersaulted backwards, 'Jack, is that you?'

And if Jack, then why not Ronnie? Would it be so extraordinary, given what he'd given his life to?

'Hello, Evie. It's been a while. Here I am. Here we are.'

She is feeling very tired. The evening is fading outside. The leaves on the crab-apple are losing their colour. She hasn't put on any lights and even her own face in the mirror seems ghostly. And was that really *him* she'd seen behind her? She might just take a nap, a little nap. Such a demanding day. She takes off her blouse and skirt and leaves them in a puddle on the chair. She slips under the duvet as if under a receiving wave.

She drifts off to sleep very quickly, but before she does—or perhaps it's a dream—she puts out an arm and feels the warm familiar weight. So it's all right, everything is all right, he's still there.